THE WAGER

Captain Tom Mason of Homicide has a peculiarly horrible case to deal with. He investigates a murder where the victim has been decapitated. However, only the body remains at the crime scene. The murderer appears to have taken the head as a grisly trophy. Prompt police action, as they cordon off the area, yields four suspects. One of them, identified as running from the scene, is held in custody — but then another three people are decapitated . . .

E. C. TUBB

---◆---

THE
WAGER

Complete and Unabridged

LINFORD
Leicester

Gloucestershire County
Council

British Library CIP Data

Tubb, E. C.
    The wager. - - (Linford mystery library)
    1. Detective and mystery stories
    2. Large type books.
    I. Title II. Series
    823.9′14–dc23

ISBN 978–1–4448–1115–5

Published by
F. A. Thorpe (Publishing)
Anstey, Leicestershire

Set by Words & Graphics Ltd.
Anstey, Leicestershire
Printed and bound in Great Britain by
T. J. International Ltd., Padstow, Cornwall

This book is printed on acid-free paper

Acknowledgements

The Wager first appeared in *Science Fantasy* for November 1955

The Ethical Assassin first appeared in *Authentic Science Fiction* for June 1955

Wishful Thinking first appeared in *Authentic Science Fiction* for July 1956

Lawyer At Large first appeared in *New Worlds* for December 1955

THE WAGER

1

It had been raining and the streets were still wet. The big car skidded a little as it swung around corners, the squeal of its tyres mingling with the wail of its siren. On the front of the vehicle a red spotlight flared with intermittent life while the two big headlamps signalled its coming from a mile away.

It slewed around a corner, tore down a tree-lined road, and skidded to a halt beside a huddled knot of men. Captain Tom Mason, Homicide, swung open the front door and stepped out of the faint smell of rubber and burnt petrol into the clean air of the rain-washed night.

'Stick around,' he said to the driver. 'If anything comes over the radio let me know.' He turned as a man walked towards him. 'Clancy?'

'Yes, sir.' The uniformed policeman touched the peak of his cap. 'You made good time, Captain.'

'Nine minutes.' Mason didn't look at his watch. 'The rest of the boys here?'

'Yes, sir. They got here about three minutes ago.'

'I was on the other side of town.' Mason hunched the collar of his shabby raincoat higher around his neck. 'Did you find the body?'

'Yes, sir. You want to see it?'

'Later. What's your story?'

'I must have missed the killer by not more than a few seconds.' Clancy sounded disgusted. 'I was on the regular beat, coming up Third and Vine and along Pine Avenue. I heard a yell and saw someone running. I grabbed him and he told me that he'd just seen a murder. I investigated and phoned in right away.'

'Pine Avenue? That's this street, isn't it?'

'That's right.'

'Where were you when you heard the yell?'

'Just coming out of Third and Vine. About a hundred yards down the avenue. I ran straight here.'

'And the witness?'

'I've got him. You want to see him?'

'Later. Did you see anything else? Hear anything?'

'No, sir. The night was quiet, we don't get much noise in this section, and the yell was all I heard.' Clancy shifted on his feet. 'It's pretty dark along here, the Avenue is only built up along one side, but I didn't see anything.'

'Not surprising.' Mason stared towards the huddle of men. Flashbulbs flickered like summer lightning and, from the distance, he heard the straining engine of a car. He looked at the officer.

'When the reporters get here keep them off my neck. Tell them I'll have a statement for them later. They can get it at Headquarters.' He smiled thinly at the officer's expression. 'Don't worry, Clancy, you'll get your picture in the papers.'

'That doesn't interest me, sir.'

'No? Then you're the first cop I've met it doesn't.' He looked around as the driver of his car came towards him.

'Reports from the roadblocks, sir. They're holding four suspects.'

'Good. Have them brought here to me.

Tell the patrols to search this area. Stop and question everyone they see. Take names and addresses, identification, the usual thing. Hold everyone who cannot or will not account for himself.' He waited until the man had returned to the car and then stepped towards the huddled knot of men.

Prentice, his assistant, came towards him. 'Almost finished, Tom. Want the details?'

'Yes.'

'The deceased is a Roger Gorman. About forty-five. Well dressed and wearing a light gabardine raincoat. Gloves, stick, soft hat, ring on the little finger of his left hand, gold wristwatch, fat wallet. You get the picture?'

'Yes.'

'Cards in the wallet says that he was a member of the Prestonville Chamber of Commerce. A couple of photographs of what could be his wife and kid. Driving licence; Lodge membership cards, business cards, a hotel key, the Grand Union, some other stuff not important as yet. You can check it all later back at Headquarters.'

'Get on with it,' said Mason tiredly. 'What else?'

'Nothing much as yet. The killer was obviously a maniac and I've sent word to check any escapes from the mental homes. I . . . '

'What makes you think he was killed by a maniac?'

'You'll see. It wasn't robbery, the wallet is intact. He was from out of town and could hardly have had local enemies. He seemed to be a decent, normal business type out for a walk before turning in. The hotel is just a few blocks from here. I've sent a man to collect his luggage.'

'You've figured all this out in, how long?'

'About five minutes.' Prentice looked pleased with himself. 'Not bad, uh?'

'Not good either. You've been reading too much. Sherlock Holmes went out with gas lighting.' He looked around. 'Where's that witness Clancy told me he had?'

'Waiting in the car. You want to see him?'

'Not yet.' He sighed. 'I suppose I'd

better look at the body now.'

He moved forward, Prentice at his side, and halted beside something covered with a rubber sheet. An officer stood by it and, as he saw Mason, he stopped and lifted the sheet from what lay underneath it. Mason stared down, his face impassive, and Prentice swung the beam from a flashlight he carried onto the corpse.

'See? I told you that it was the work of a maniac.'

'Or someone trying to give us that impression?' Mason didn't look at his assistant. Hardened as he was to crime and the inhumanity of man towards man, yet he had never grown to relish the sight of death. Privately he considered it to be the worst part of his job and, staring down at what lay revealed in the light of the flashlight, he found nothing to alter his opinion. It wasn't just that the man was dead, it was what had been done to the corpse.

It didn't have a head.

★   ★   ★

The witness was a human derelict stinking of cheap wine and redolent with dirt. He blinked up at Mason and ran the tip of his tongue between snags of teeth. His clothing was damp and he looked half-numbed as though things were happening too fast for him. He didn't look towards where the body lay.

'You saw the actual murder?' Mason shivered slightly in his thin raincoat. He knew that all this questioning could have been done in the comfort of Headquarters but he had a theory that first impressions were valuable and he wanted to get all the facts before witness and suspects had time to forget or alter what they knew and had seen.

'Well,' the witness seemed doubtful, 'I didn't really see it. I was sitting down and heard something and when I looked up there was a man on the ground and another man was running away.'

'In which direction?'

'That way.' The witness pointed to the unlit side of the avenue. 'He was tall and ran like he was scared or something. I was still looking after him when the cop arrived.'

'Did you shout?'

'No.'

'Did you make any sound at all? Did you call to the man, for example?'

'Not me.'

'That sound you heard, what was it? A cry for help? A scream?'

'I don't know,' said the man. He belched. 'I was asleep and it must've woke me up. I saw the fellow though.'

'Which one?'

'The one running away, like I told you.'

'Would you know him again?'

'I don't know.' The man looked cunning. 'I reckon so. Witnesses get paid, don't they?'

'Not for lying,' said Mason curtly. 'Would you know him again if you saw him?'

'I reckon so. In this light anyway. I wouldn't know about in a room.'

'It won't be in a room.' Mason stared towards where Prentice was ushering four people towards him. 'Stay here. Watch those people. If you recognise anyone let me know. Don't speak and don't move. Understand?'

The witness nodded and Mason walked towards the four people. The first suspect was quickly cleared. He was a small, balding, nervous man. He plucked at Mason's sleeve and whispered something. The Captain frowned. 'Speak up. You all know why you are here. A crime has been committed and all I want to know is who you are, where you were going, who can vouch for you. Once cleared you can go home.' He looked down at the little man. 'Well?'

'It's my wife, Captain. I didn't want her to know where I was. My name is Blake, Edward Blake, and I can prove where I was from nine o'clock until when the officer stopped me.'

'Where were you?'

'At Madame Cormay's.' The little man blushed. 'You know how it is, Captain.'

'I know,' said Mason. He had heard of the notorious Madame Cormay. One day the vice squad was going to do the work they were paid to do and she would be put out of business. He gestured towards an officer. 'Take this man and check his story. Take him home and check where he lives. You know what to do.' He looked at the remaining three suspects. Two were men the third a woman. She clung to the hand of one of the men and Mason guessed that they were together.

They were and their story was simple. They were married, but not to each other, and for obvious reasons they didn't want any investigations made at their respective homes. Mason sent them off with two officers and left it to them to make up their own alibis. He stared at the remaining man.

'Your name?'

'Holden. Gort Holden.'

'Address?'

'Central Plaza.'

'All right, Mr. Holden. You heard what I said to the others. As you live in a hotel I'm afraid that I just can't send you home with an officer. That wouldn't prove anything. If you'll just let me know whom to contact to vouch for you I won't detain you any longer.' He paused, waiting, then as the man made no move held out his hand. 'Give.'

'Give you what?'

'Your papers. Your wallet, identity, social security card, anything and everything which will prove to me who and what you are.'

'I'm afraid that I can't do that.'

'Can't or won't?'

'Can't, sorry.' Gort smiled and made as though to walk away. Mason stopped him, his fingers hard on the other's arm.

'Not so fast. Maybe if you see why I'm so interested in you you'll change your mind.' Mason gestured to an officer. 'Take this man and show him. Bring him back afterwards to me.' He waited until the couple had moved off then looked towards the witness. The man grinned and nodded his head.

When Gort returned he looked pale and almost physically ill. He stood for a moment gulping at the rain-washed air and in the light of the street lamps, his eyes looked haggard.

'You should have warned me,' he said. 'That man! It's horrible!'

'Sorry.' Mason didn't feel regret. 'That man was murdered a short while ago. The murderer was seen making his escape. We blocked all roads and are checking the vicinity and all people who fail to identify themselves. I take it that you have no serious objection to being identified?'

'By the person who saw the murderer? Of course not.'

'I didn't exactly mean that,' said Mason gently. 'There must be someone who would vouch for you. Your employer? Your family? Your associates?'

'Naturally.' Gort hesitated. 'But is that necessary? Surely if you have a witness to the crime he could clear me?'

'Perhaps.' In the dim light the captain's face was enigmatic. 'You have no objection if we try?'

'Of course not.'

'I see.' Mason turned to the witness who had approached while they were talking. 'Well? Is this the man you saw?'

'Could be.' The man swayed closer and Gort recoiled from the sour odour of his breath. 'Yes, that's the man.'

'Are you positive?'

'Well . . . ' The hesitation was obvious. 'The light was bad and my eyes ain't none too good, but I'd say he's the one.

Same shaped head. Same height and the same colour clothing. He's your man all right.'

'Impossible!' Gort thrust himself towards the witness. 'You've never seen me before in your whole life. You are mistaken.' He appealed to Mason. 'You can't believe this man. He would say anything if he thought that it would please you.'

'Maybe.' Mason nodded towards an officer. 'But it's eye-witness testimony against your unsupported denial. I'm afraid that I shall have to hold you for further investigation.'

He turned back to the corpse as the officer led Gort away.

2

To Gort the whole thing seemed like a wild fantasy. He sat on a hard, narrow cot in a small, concrete room and stared at a tiny patch of blue sky high against one wall. The cell was cramped, primitive, and utterly bleak to a man used to the comforts of a galactic-wide civilisation. And the worst part of it all was that nothing he could do would save him. Intelligence, even that of a high order, couldn't combat iron bars and stone walls.

And he was beginning to doubt his own intelligence.

Arrest had meant a bath, not that that mattered, his camouflage was proof against anything but the special solvents but, at the same time, that camouflage wasn't a permanent fixture and would need touching up from time to time. He had retained the clothing he had worn at the time of the arrest, and thinking of that clothing made him writhe with anger at his stupidity. To have worn it at all had been ridiculous. He should never have discarded his own special garments because, without them, he was helpless.

The thought of just how utter that helplessness was made him squirm.

He looked up as the door opened and Mason entered the cell. He waited until the door had been locked behind him then sat on the single chair and faced Gort.

'Well? Have you changed your mind yet?'

Gort didn't answer. He knew what the captain wanted, proof of his identity, but that very proof was the one thing he couldn't give. There wasn't a man or woman on the face of this planet who could vouch for him. There was absolutely no paper proof of his birth, education, employment, medical history, none of the thousand and one records normal to anyone living in this particular hemisphere.

'We've checked the Central Plaza and all they can tell us is that you booked in a week ago, two days before your arrest We've searched your things without result. It isn't good enough.' He paused, waiting for Gort to speak.

'What else can I do?' Gort knew the answer and knew that he couldn't help.

'I've told you that more than once,' said Mason wearily. 'Who are you? Where do you normally live? Where do you work? Have you any friends of good standing who can vouch for you?' He made an expressive gesture of impatience. 'Don't think that I want to keep you here, I don't, but I can't release you until I know just who and what you are. Want to tell me?'

'I . . . ' Gort swallowed and shook his head. The situation was impossible. The truth wouldn't be believed and, if it were, it would be the last thing he dared tell. For the first time he began to fully appreciate the warning he had been given.

'Never underestimate them,' Rhubens had said. 'They're ignorant, stupid, illogical but they have their own brand of native cunning. Once they get hold of an idea they never stop worrying at it until they find an answer. It needn't be the correct answer, but they want one just the same.' The commander had laughed with easy good humour. 'There's no need to warn you of the females but be careful of their law enforcement. They're fanatically security-conscious and they'll disregard ethics and everything else if they become the slightest bit suspicious.'

That had been eight days ago and he was only now beginning to realise what the commander had meant.

'The position,' said Mason grimly, 'is this. A man has been murdered in a particularly horrible way. Every other suspect in the area has been vouched for and is clear. You are the only possible suspect and, even more important, you have been identified by a witness. I hate to say this but, unless you decide to cooperate, you're heading straight for the electric chair. It's up to you to clear yourself if you want to avoid it.'

'Wait a moment.' Gort frowned as he tried to recall all he had learned. 'Isn't there something about a man being innocent until found guilty?'

'There is,' admitted the captain dryly. 'But I shouldn't count on it if I were you.'

'Then what about the evidence? I had no weapon. My clothes were clean and, above all, I wasn't carrying the . . . ' Gort felt a recurrence of his sickness as he tried to say the word.

'The head?' Mason looked thoughtful. 'That's right you weren't, were you.'

'Then the evidence alone should clear me. You have no real justification for detaining me at all.'

'No?' Mason shrugged. 'I don't agree with you.' He stared curiously at the man on the bunk. 'Have you any Indian blood?'

'What?' Gort realised that he didn't know what the captain was driving at. 'No, I don't think so. Why?'

'You've been here five days now and the warder tells me that you haven't shaved once during that time. Pure Indians don't have to shave, they just don't grow whiskers.' Mason scrubbed at his own chin. 'Lucky devils. You're a vegetarian too, aren't you?'

'I don't eat flesh,' said Gort cautiously. 'Is that what you mean?'

'That's right.' Mason rose and stared down at his prisoner. 'But you're the first vegetarian I've ever met who refuses to eat meat, fish, eggs and any product of any animal. That must account for the way you felt when you saw the body. You should have warned me that you had a weak stomach.'

Gort snatched at the opportunity. 'I can't stand the sight of blood,' he said. 'Doesn't that prove my innocence?'

'Sorry, but no.' Mason banged on the door for the warder to come and let him out. 'If you want to do that you'd better start talking and you'd better do it fast. Public opinion has been aroused and, if you leave it too late, you may find yourself in the position of not being believed. Think it over.'

The door closed behind him and, alone once more, Gort stretched himself full-length on the bunk. The warning had been very plain. Clear yourself — or be used as a scapegoat. Desperately he racked his brains for some way out of this almost ludicrous situation. For a man who could repair an instantaneous warp-drive, who had an intelligence at least five times that of the brightest inhabitant of this world and who was a member of the Guardians, to be confined on a false accusation in a primitive jail was something he didn't like to think about.

He could hire a lawyer he supposed, they would allow him to use his money for that purpose, but a lawyer would want to know all about him and so he would be no better off. If he could get his clothing he stood a chance, Mason had said that they had been searched but the woven-in circuits and power source had been designed to avoid detection. But before he could get his clothes he would have to clear himself and . . .

Restlessly he sat up and stared at the window high above his head. With a smooth co-ordination of muscle he jumped and drew himself up so that his face was pressed against the bars. From his vantage point he could see the roof of a building opposite, a few fleecy clouds, and an expanse of clear blue sky. He stared at the sky for a long time and, somehow, the sight began to irritate him. Up there was all the help he needed or could possibly use.

But he wasn't up there.

3

Heltin wasn't satisfied with the ship but it was the best Jelkson would provide. He wasn't satisfied with his partner either, but it was a case of take it or leave it and Heltin, with expensive tastes and a liking for the dubious pleasures of the Rim worlds, had had no choice. Now he sat in the control chair and looked at the image on the screens.

'Is that it?' San Luchin leaned over the pilot's shoulder his cat-eyes blazing with anticipation. Heltin nodded.

'That's it. The quarry planet. Are your people ready?'

'Certainly. We have arranged a most ingenious wager. You will drop us at the same point as where I obtained the last trophy. You will give us three revolutions and then pick us up again. The one who has collected the greatest number of trophies will win twenty thousand milars.' He inhaled with a peculiar sibilance. 'It should be good sport.'

'Don't make it too good,' warned Heltin uneasily. 'You've been here before and you know that these things have a civilisation of sorts. It could be that you may find yourselves in serious trouble. It isn't just a question of landing and reaping a harvest, you know. The whole object is to pit your wits and skill against the inhabitants — and get away with it.' He hesitated. 'Are you certain that you wouldn't prefer a more isolated area?'

'No.' San Luchin was very positive. 'The entire attraction of the plan is that we shall be in some personal danger. We are taking only the essential protection-equipment and must use our full skill both to obtain the trophies and to escape detection. You have a hypno-tutor for the language?'

'Yes, the settings are ready in place. I couldn't get much local currency though, you'll have to make out the best you can.' Heltin adjusted the controls and the image on the screens suddenly jerked into close proximity. 'Hurry up with your preparations. I don't want to hang around here longer than I have to.'

'Why not? The Guardians can't spot your screens, can they?'

'I hope not,' said Heltin feelingly. 'That base on the moon looks awfully efficient to me.'

He slid the vessel closer to the planet as his passengers familiarised themselves with the language, and, judging the time to a nicety, he landed when the sun was on the other side of the planet. Cautiously, he opened the air lock and stared at the darkness outside.

A man, walking along the deserted street stared at the bulk of the ship then continued on his way. Heltin grinned, the invisibility screens were obviously doing their job and for a moment he was tempted to leave the vessel where it was rather than follow his original plan of waiting beneath the surface of one of the seas. He dismissed the notion. Even though the local inhabitants couldn't spot him, yet the Guardians might just be able to spot his radiation and, even with his altered screens, it would be wiser to shield himself with a mile of ocean. He turned as his passengers crowded towards the air lock.

San Luchin took the lead. He, like all the rest, wore something so near to the native clothing as to be unnoticeable. Each had camouflaged his personal characteristics and each carried a single offensive weapon, of a low order of efficiency and yet one ideally suited to the project in hand. Heltin watched as the five men dropped to the ground.

'Wait a minute,' he said sharply. 'You've forgotten something. What are you going to keep them in?'

'That is our affair,' San Luchin expressed his irritation with a peculiar gesture, a tensing and clawing of the right hand. 'We intend to enjoy the sport to the full and the harder we can make it the better it will be. Take off now and return for us in three revolutions.'

Heltin shrugged. 'It's your party. Good hunting.'

They nodded and moved away as the door slid shut. Before they had cleared the immediate area the ship had flickered from view and a moment later a rush of air told that it had left. San Luchin held a quick council.

'I suggest we separate to divergent areas,' he said in the newly acquired language. 'Aside from force jackets we shall be defenceless and, in order to prevent interference, we shall make no attempt at personal contact until we meet here at the appointed time. Agreed?'

They nodded and moved away, each taking a route as well away from the others as possible. San Luchin watched them go then, after a moment's thought, made his way towards the centre of town.

He hummed a little as he walked, a soft, almost feral purring of the breath and his eyes, as he stared at the surrounding crowds, glowed with mounting anticipation. He had been right to insist on a three-revolution stay. He had been right to make the hunt as severe as possible. For too long now there had been no real opportunity for good sport. Even the manufactured androids were but a poor substitute for the real thing. They were good, but they could only be as good as the builders made them and, once you had built a thing, you knew its exact capabilities. These things were different. Their capabilities were unknown and might prove to be delightfully dangerous.

He restrained the subconscious movement of his hand towards the weapon beneath his jacket. Not yet. The taking of trophies would be the easy part even though it was the ultimate thrill. He could afford to wait and enjoy the pleasure of anticipation. First there were other things to attend to, the finding of a hide, the watching of the quarry, the obtaining of the cache. The humming grew louder as he stepped carefully through the crowds.

He hadn't enjoyed himself so much for years.

4

Captain Mason sat in his office and stared at the litter of papers before him. It was night and a desk lamp threw a broad cone of light over the scattered sheets. Reports mostly, details of a search, which, so far, had proven useless. He picked up a file and began to riffle the pages looking for the thousandth time for something, he didn't know what, to give him a clue to the most publicised murder for the past ten years.

He looked up as the assistant D.A. slammed into the room and helped himself to a chair.

'Still at it, Tom?'

'Still at it.' Mason sighed and accepted the cigarette the other man offered. 'Thanks. Going ahead with the trial, Bob?'

'What else can we do?' Bob Shaw thumbed a lighter and lit the cigarettes. 'The old man's out on a limb. The press is riding him hard and, unless he clears up this case he can kiss his chances in the coming election goodbye.'

'You think that you can get a conviction?'

'It's a certainty.' Bob stared at the lined face of the captain. 'What's the matter? Don't you believe that Holden did it?'

'I'm not certain he did,' admitted Mason slowly. 'Somehow it just doesn't add up.' He picked up the file. 'No motive. No weapon. No stains on his clothing. He could just have been walking down the road as he claims when we picked him up.'

'You're forgetting the witness,' reminded Shaw. 'He's willing to swear that Holden is the man he saw running from the scene of the crime.'

'That wino? Who'd believe him?'

'The jury will, and that's all that matters.' Shaw dragged at his cigarette. 'He broken down yet?'

'Not yet.'

'That won't help him either. Playing dumb isn't the right way to prove innocence. If you've got nothing to hide then why not speak up? Quit feeling sorry for him, Tom, if he's in trouble then it's his own fault.'

'Maybe.' Mason sighed as he put down the file. 'I'm still not happy about it though. You haven't really got a case against him at all. Any good lawyer could rip it apart and get it thrown out of court.'

'You think so?' Shaw blew smoke through his nose. 'I don't agree. Look, we can forget the motive angle. The dead man was a bit of a playboy and we can suggest that our friend was a little jealous or something. That part doesn't matter. The man's dead that's all we've got to worry about, and Holden's a sitting duck to take the rap.'

'Even if he's innocent?'

'Tell that to the birds. He's as guilty as hell, that's why he clammed up, he knows that as soon as he starts talking we're going to check and trip him up.' Shaw stared at Mason. 'Listen. He threw the knife away, that's simple, there's a big piece of waste ground right next to where the killing took place and it's got a storm drain at the end of it. He dumped his cargo too, doubled back, and then tried to make out he was only taking a walk. It was his bad luck he was seen by a witness and that we managed to cordon the area so soon. Five more minutes and he would have got clean away.'

'And the blood?'

'Luck or . . . ' Bob shrugged. 'We'll settle for luck.' He rose, to his feet. 'Did you get anywhere with his prints?'

'No. They aren't on file anywhere.'

'Maybe he's a draft dodger too,' suggested Bob. 'Anyway, don't let it get you down, Tom. After all, what's it to you?' He left and the captain frowned down at the file again.

It was easy for Bob to talk, easier still for him to sit back and be cynical even if it sent an innocent man to the chair, but Mason couldn't forget that an officer's duty wasn't just to assume guilt, he should also help to prove innocence.

And something was wrong.

He knew it. He felt it every time he saw the prisoner. The man wasn't insane, and what sane man would decapitate another? He wasn't even a killer, though Mason knew that any man given the right conditions could become a killer. It was something intangible, something not quite fitting into the correct groove and, the more he thought about it, the more it began to worry him.

The fingerprints for example. Holden had been printed as a matter of routine and his prints sent to the agencies for checking. That they weren't on file wasn't too extraordinary, it merely meant that he had never worked in a defence plant, been previously arrested, served with the armed forces, worked for a big company, or applied for a passport. What was extraordinary was the prints themselves.

Mason stared at them, frowning at the strange, utterly unnatural pattern. He knew that all normal prints fell into defined categories depending on the arches and whorls but Holden's were in a class by themselves. No arches, no whorls, a series of herringbone patterns overlaid by a writhing mass of circular lines, the whole blurred and distorted to an almost unrecognisable extent. It was puzzling and mentally Mason began reviewing the case against Gort.

The knife? Shaw had explained that and, if the crime had been premeditated, that was just what the murderer would have done. Motive? Unessential, it wasn't his job to prove motive. The blood? Luck as Shaw had said, or . . . ?

The blood!

Hastily Mason thumbed through the file until he found what he was looking for, an eight by ten blowup of the scene of the crime. He squinted at it, something nagging at his brain then, with quick impatience, flipped the switch on an intercom.

'Desk? Mason here. Get me Doc Wheelan.' He waited, fingers drumming on the edge of his desk. 'Doc? Mason here. How much blood does a body contain?' He frowned at the sounds coming from the speaker. 'No, I'm not joking, this could be serious.' He listened again. 'That much? If someone were to slash off a head would it spurt out? Most of it? Depends? Look, you know the case I'm working on? Well, as far as I can tell from the photographs there was hardly any blood at all. How do you account for that?' He listened again. 'O.K. O.K., so I didn't notice it at the time. Hell, Doc, it was raining, the night was dark and I had other things on my mind. The report? No, I didn't read it, why should I have done? The man was dead, wasn't he, and even I could see the cause. Can you boil it down?' Mason's face hardened as he listened to the voice from the speaker. 'Are you certain? You are? O.K., Doc, keep your shirt on. I only wanted to know.'

Slowly he broke the connection, his face heavy with thought then, abruptly, he threw the switch again.

'Desk? Mason here. Bring down the prisoner Gort Holden. Bring him down right away.'

He waited staring down at the photograph, the crease between his eyes a living question mark.

* * *

The simplicity of it was such that Gort felt utterly ashamed of not having thought of it before. In order to escape he needed his special clothing so, as he was still not in prison garb and wouldn't be until after the trial, he deliberately destroyed the clothes he was wearing. The warder had shrugged when he saw the wreckage and, as the prisoner had more clothes of his own, what was simpler than to fetch them?

It was as easy as that.

Dressed once more in his protective clothing. Gort felt a new man. He sat on the edge of the bunk and wondered just what would be best for him to do. He could slice out the bars of the window and float out to freedom. He could cut the lock from the door and get out that way. He could generate the force-field which would protect him from all missile and most energy weapons and nothing these people could do would stop him. He could also trip the emergency signal and call to the base for help.

But to do any of these things would be both an admission of failure and betrayal of his trust.

First, he had aroused enough suspicion

as it was without arousing more. Calling for help now was both unnecessary and unjustified and, if he did, he would have some awkward questions to answer when he got back to base. A Guardian, even a young one, was supposed to be able to use his own initiative. Sitting on the edge of the bunk he decided to do nothing for the time being. Being able to escape any time he wanted to made all the difference and, even though he didn't like to admit it, his recent experience had taught him a lot.

It had taught him that a man was only as good as his technology. Even with his high intelligence, his so-called superiority over these primitives, yet he had been helpless without his gadgets. In a way he'd been even worse than the natives because they didn't tend to rely on force-fields and all the other appurtenances common to his own civilisation. It was a sobering thought and he was still brooding over it when the warder came to take him to Mason.

The captain wasted no time.

'There's something funny about you

Holden and I want to know what it is. There's another matter too . . . ' His voice trailed off as he glanced at the photograph. 'But never mind that for now.' He dropped the glossy print and gestured to a chair. 'Sit down.'

Gort sat down. Strangely enough he didn't feel in the slightest bit upset. Maybe it was because he now knew himself to be invulnerable or it may have been that, for the first time since his arrest, he was beginning to enjoy himself.

'Do you still refuse to give me data about yourself?' Mason asked the question as though he didn't really expect an answer and, for a moment, Gort was tempted to tell him the truth. He resisted the insane impulse, this was no time for joking.

'I do.'

'Then let me tell you something about yourself.' Mason relaxed in his chair and stared at his prisoner. 'You may not have known it but you've been under constant surveillance since your arrest. For example we know that you have never once shaved. You have never eaten any product of any dead or living animal and, as far as we can determine, you have never slept.' He stared thoughtfully at Gort. 'Another thing, your fingerprints aren't normal. I have never seen a pattern like them before and I think that it's safe to say another such pattern does not exist.' He leaned forward his eyes suspicious.

'What are you, Holden?'

Not who, *what*! The significance of the word sent a chill up Gort's spine. Mason was suspicious, maybe it was only the vague glimmerings of an idea as yet but, remembering Rhubens' advice, Gort knew that he dared take no chances. He smiled.

'What? You mean who, don't you?'

'Perhaps.' Mason didn't elaborate. 'Are you going to talk?'

'I can tell you a few things,' said Gort. 'I don't know why I have no need to shave. I've never thought about it before, it's just one of those things, you know how it is.'

'Do I?'

'Well, you said yourself that Indians never had to shave so what's so peculiar about it?' Gort gestured with his hands.

'I'm a vegetarian, yes, I've never denied it but that's no crime. I just don't like eating dead tissue or the products of living organisms. I may be fanatical on the subject but my stomach's my own.'

'And the sleeplessness?'

'That's nonsense,' lied Gort. 'I sleep just the same as anyone else but I've trained myself to take my rest in snatches. I'll drop off for ten minutes or half an hour, wake up for a few minutes, then drop off again.' He smiled. 'I've got a theory about it.'

Mason didn't smile. 'You still haven't told me anything,' he reminded. 'Do you want to be tried for murder?'

'You won't convict me,' said Gort positively. 'I'm innocent.' He looked at the photograph. 'Is that the scene of the crime?'

'Yes,' Mason picked it up, hesitated, then handed it to Gort. 'You might be able to help me. When you saw the body did you notice any blood?'

'Blood?' Gort paused, the photograph in his hand. 'I can't remember, is it important?'

'It could be,' said Mason seriously.

'Something odd has come up and I want to be certain that I'm right. If you could remember it would help a lot.'

Gort nodded and threw his mind back to recall the incident. He concentrated and suddenly, he could smell the rain-wet night, hear the soft sounds made by the shoes of the men, see the huddled and headless figure sprawled on the grass. He controlled his revulsion and forced himself to scan the area.

'There was a little blood at the upper limit of the corpse,' he said carefully. 'Is that what you want to know?'

'How much blood?' Then, as Gort hesitated. 'A smear or two, a pint, a gallon? Was the grass covered with it or was it only in one small area?'

'There wasn't a lot. Just a heavy smear on the grass.'

'Yes,' said Mason heavily. 'That's what I thought.' He stared at Gort. 'I've just read the medical report and spoken to the doctor. It appears that the head was removed with an incredibly sharp instrument, which apparently had the power to cauterise the wound as it cut. The single smear of blood apparently came from a minor wound caused after death. I use the word 'apparently' because, as far as we know, no such instrument exists.' He paused and stared at Gort. 'Just as fingerprints such as yours do not exist.'

'But they do,' said Gort and held up his hands. 'I have them.'

'Exactly.' Mason reached for his intercom. 'You needn't worry about being put on trial for murder. I am going to inform Security and you will be held for further questioning. I'm sorry, Holden, but you realise that I cannot chance the fact that you may be a spy.'

The phone jangled just as he was about to speak and, with an irritated expression, he lifted the receiver. 'Mason here. What is it?'

Watching him Gort could see his expression change from irritation to incredulity. 'What! Three of them? Where?' He listened, one hand making swift notations on the pad before him. 'All without heads? Wait! Any blood? You don't know? Check on it then, and hurry!'

His eyes met those of Gort and, as if

the sight had reminded him of something, he reached again for the intercom. The squawking of the phone interrupted him for a second time.

'No blood? Are you positive? Good. Yes, I'll be right over. Yes, looks like the same man at work again. Cordon the area and proceed as usual.'

Mason slammed down the receiver, reached for the intercom, then slumped in sudden immobility.

Gort rose. He had about half a minute to make his escape, the paralysis wouldn't last longer than that for fear of causing death, but before he went he had something to do. Quickly he wiped the photograph, took the officer's wallet card from his pocket and, with easy strides, moved towards the door.

A second application of the paralysis vibration cleared his path and, before Mason could recover, he was in the street and on his way to freedom. Almost he felt sorry for the captain but what else could he have done? A more rigorous confinement would have necessitated the loss of his protective clothing and all hope of escape. As it was he had merely walked out leaving unanswered questions. Mason, no matter what his suspicions, couldn't now verify them.

Gort was free to continue his interrupted vacation.

5

San Luchin sat in his hotel room and trembled as he listened to the newscast. The fools! The unutterable fools to have gone trophy hunting so soon after arrival. And yet, fools though they were, their action had made the hunt even more exciting.

A large-scale map of the city was spread before him on the floor and he scanned it, marking the areas where the bodies had been found, his cat-eyes blazing with interest as he extrapolated the probable results of the mistimed hunting. Obviously they had underestimated the resources of this planet According to the newscast the areas were now cordoned and every person discovered within them would be questioned and examined. Equally obvious they would have to discard their trophies and, at the same time, run a risk of discovery.

He bared his teeth as he thought about

it, almost envying them their position, and yet, at the same time recognising their danger. Not of personal annihilation, of course, their protective force-fields would safeguard them from that, but of their being kept so busy that they would inevitably lose the wager. Also, and this was most important, they had to avoid all unnecessary suspicion. Not that the natives mattered, they didn't, but the watchful Guardians did and this was too fine a quarry planet for them to lose it so soon.

The foolish part had been in taking trophies where the bodies were certain to be almost immediately discovered.

Restlessly he began to pace the floor. His own plans were made, he had scanned the area, knew just where and when to strike, and even had his containers for his trophies ready and waiting. He paused beside the plastic suitcases — how strange that this race should know of plastics. Ideal for his purpose, they were light, strong, and of a size both designed for good capacity and lack of unessential bulk. He was still examining them when the knock came at the door.

'Yes?'

'Police, open up.'

'One moment.' Quickly he checked to make sure that his eyes were hidden by contact lenses, his camouflage perfect and his clothing adjusted. He opened the door before the uniformed officer had time to knock again.

'Can I help you?'

'You can answer some questions,' snapped the officer. He was big, broad, a holstered weapon hanging at his belt and his uniform cap pushed back on his bald skull. San Luchin stared, fascinated, at that skull, mentally imagining it mounted on the wall of his trophy room, and wondered again at the incredible variety of trophies it was possible to obtain on this planet. He remembered to smile.

'Certainly. What would you like to know?'

'Where were you during the past two hours? Have you any identity? Is there anyone who can vouch for you?' The officer droned the questions and San

Luchin guessed that he was merely conducting a routine investigation. He relaxed a little and reached inside his jacket for a wallet.

'Here, driver's licence, social security card, lodge membership cards and insurance policy. I'm a stranger in town, drove in on business, and I've kept pretty well to my room for the past few hours.' He smiled again. 'Got a touch of flu, I guess. The receptionist should be able to verify that.'

'I've already checked,' said the officer. He stared at the papers the wallet contained. 'Sorry to trouble you Mr. Jones, but you know how it is on this job. With a maniac prowling the city we just can't be too careful.' He closed the wallet and handed it back. 'If you ask me this is a waste of time. Hell, anyone would know that the killer wouldn't hang around the scene of his operations. Anyway, what's the good of checking every resident just for suspicious characters?'

'It must be hard on you,' sympathised San Luchin. He knew better than to be dogmatic. 'Think you'll find them?'

'Them?' The officer raised his eyebrows. 'Who said anything about 'them'?'

It had been a mistake but he hadn't been able to resist the deliberate provocation. A good hunter learns the reactions of his quarry and San Luchin knew himself to be a good hunter. He forced himself to look away from that tempting trophy.

'Sorry, I guess that I was getting confused. Three bodies, you know . . . ' He gestured with his hands. The officer nodded.

'That's right, but there can only be one killer nutty enough to do what he did.' He slid back his cap and scratched his naked scalp. 'Well, guess that I'd better be getting on with the job. Goodnight, Mr. Jones.'

'Goodnight.' San Luchin leaned against the closed door and gulped at the thick, slightly arid air. Desperately he fought to control his reactions. Not yet! Not yet! Not yet! The thought hammered within his skull and gradually calmed the seething emotions within him. Almost he had yielded to temptation and he had a momentary glimpse of precognition. The trophy taken, then the inevitable flight, the hunt in which the hunter would be the hunted. The pitting of wits against wits, skill against skill, and all the time there would be the temptation to acquire more and more trophies. He closed his eyes and quivered in orgiastic mental pleasure.

When he opened them again he was ice calm.

★   ★   ★

The others had yielded to temptation and were now probably devoid of hides, trophies and caches. In effect they would have had to start again with the handicap of wasted time. As strangers in the city they would be suspect and . . .

He was also a stranger.

The wallet had been taken from a native he had met and killed for the single purpose of establishing his hide. The body he had hidden in thick undergrowth at the edge of the city trusting to luck that it would not be discovered and its identity established too soon. Now, because of the general suspicion, it was almost certain that very thing would happen.

The officer had been tired but these things were, in their way, remarkably efficient. He would remember the name, the foreign accent, the mistake of the word 'them'. The hotel receptionist too might begin to wonder about the strange guest who stayed close to his room. A part of his mind told him that he was worrying unnecessarily but another part, the cold, calculating hunter's part, warned him constantly of the danger of under-estimation. He was still undecided when the officer returned to his room.

This time he didn't knock, but walked straight in, and San Luchin cursed the carelessness that had made him forget to lock the door.

'What do you want?'

'Just one more question.' The officer's eyes slid around the room. 'You said that you drove into town on business?'

'That's right.'

'What sort of business?'

'Pedlar.' San Luchin saw at once that

he had chosen the wrong word. 'I sell things.'

'A drummer.' The officer nodded. 'What's your line?'

'Cases, suitcases.' The cache gave its own answer. 'Satisfied?'

'Sure,' the officer fumbled at his note-book. 'Just one other thing.' He looked apologetic. 'You speak sort of funny, you know, as if you might be a foreigner or something. Are you?'

'No.' San Luchin searched his hypnoti-cally acquired knowledge of the language for semantically soothing words. 'I've an impediment, it plays hell with my trade, but the regular man's sick just now and I didn't want to lose a contract.' Sickly he realised that he was making things worse.

'So you own the business?' The officer moved towards the telephone on the bedside table. 'Good, that makes things a lot easier. I'll just check with your home town and that'll finish it. Number?'

'I've got it here,' San Luchin fumbled inside his jacket and stepped closer. Now that he knew what he had to do he felt a

53

terrible relief. Anyway, the trophy would be spectacular and, even more important, it would make the game so much more exciting.

He stepped towards the officer.

6

Gort could feel the tension of the city. People clustered in little knots and groups, their eyes suspicious as they stared at every passer-by, and the wail of sirens echoed from the high buildings as carloads of police hurried from point to point. It was late, almost midnight, but every light was on and the main streets were brilliantly lit. Gort knew that, unless he took precautions, it would only be a matter of time before he was stopped, questioned, and held for arrest. Mason must have circulated his description and every officer would be on the look out for him. He needed time to plan his next move.

An all-night restaurant flashed gaudy neon at him from across the street and he swung towards it, not feeling really at ease until the doors had swung shut behind him. The place was almost empty, a few of the high stools being occupied by morose men and blowzy women, and, after a quick look round, Gort sat in one of the booths. A waiter, his pale face as tired as his apron, wiped automatically at the table and thrust forward a fly-blown menu.

'Coffee.' Gort stared at the almost empty restaurant. 'How's business?'

'You kidding?' The waiter scowled. 'Normally the place is jumping this time of night. Late diners on their way home from the movies, transients, drifters, early-shift workers, we get 'em all. Now look at it. Much more of this and we might as well shut up for good.' He moved away to fetch the order and Gort took advantage of the privacy to check the contents of the stolen wallet.

Money, not too much but enough for immediate emergencies.

Some papers, an identification card, a badge, and the usual trivia most men carry about with them. The money would be useful, all that Gort had carried was probably still locked in the precinct safe together with his wrist watch, loose change, keys and other nonessentials. He shrugged, he could afford to lose them, they were only local products, and he could return the wallet later. He looked up as the waiter brought his coffee.

'Thanks. What's all the fuss about?'

'Don't you know?' The waiter was too tired to think it strange and was glad of the opportunity to talk. 'It's this killer that's still running around. You meant you haven't heard?'

'I'm a night-worker,' explained Gort. 'My TV's broken and I didn't get a paper. What's the latest?'

'He killed a copper, sliced off his head in a hotel room.' The waiter shook his head. 'I don't get it. That's four dead so far and all the same way.' He licked his lips with morbid interest. 'Four so far, all at different points of the city and all without heads. What the hell would he be wanting with a lot of heads? The guy must be way off the beam.'

'In a hotel room?' Gort looked thoughtful. 'They must know who he is then.'

'Some lousy foreigner from what I can make out. He skipped and they're looking for him now.' The waiter sucked at his teeth. 'They got a description, he's an odd looking character, and if he's on the streets they'll find him.' He swabbed at the table. 'Something wrong with the coffee?'

'It's cold. Fetch me some more will you, without milk this time.'

Alone, Gort considered what he had just heard. He had thought it odd that his escape had caused so much excitement then, as he remembered Mason's telephone conversation he began to understand. A city-wide search for an insane killer, obviously the same killer who had caused the original trouble — and he had walked out right into the middle of it.

The waiter brought the milkless coffee and Gort concentrated on some deep thinking.

The trouble was that these people were so suspicious. He could understand it, of course, all they had to go on was paper-proof and interchangeable identity, but that meant a tremendous amount of work in checking that each person was who he was supposed to be. Even documents weren't enough, personal relationships counted for much more and, unless a man had someone who could vouch for him, he could easily get into serious trouble. Gort had paper-proof, as Captain Mason he should be safe from unauthorised detection unless the person checking him knew the captain personally. Or, no, every policeman would have been warned of the stolen papers so, in a way, he was no better off. For a moment Gort toyed with the idea of stealing someone else's papers then, almost at once, dismissed the notion. Self-preservation was one thing but deliberate, unnecessary crime was something else. And anyway, he had no money.

Like it or not it seemed that he would have to terminate his vacation.

He didn't want to, he had been enjoying himself and he didn't know, when the opportunity would arise again for a holiday on this particular world. Educationally it had little to offer, in effect it served as an example of what a civilised world was not, and, even though he had quite a long life ahead of him, yet there were still many more worlds to see. Even Rhubens who had been stationed at the moon base for the past twenty periods had only been down once because, as he said, the stultifying effects were too grave to risk more often. Sitting at the table staring at the brown liquid before him, Gort could agree with the commander. He felt almost stupid, his brain working only with a tremendous effort, and it was quite possible that, if he stayed too long, he might seriously impair his faculties.

Which was one of the reasons why Earth was in such strict quarantine.

The waiter was hovering around again, perhaps waiting for a chance to engage in conversation or perhaps because he was suspicious. Gort rose, paid for the untouched coffee with one of the stolen bills, pocketed his change and stepped out into the street.

A man approached him as he neared a corner, a civilian fortunately, and Gort stopped.

'Going towards Edwards and Main, mister?'

'No.' Gort had memorised a map of the

city. 'Eleventh and Spring. Why?'

'We're making up a party.' The man gestured towards a car almost filled with men and women. 'It's pretty dark that way and it could be that the killer's lurking down there. If you lived that way I'd take you home for a couple of dollars. Where did you say you were heading?'

'Eleventh and Spring.'

'Then Sam could run you there.' He turned and shouted towards another man. 'Hey, Sam! Can you take one more?'

'It doesn't matter,' said Gort hastily. 'I've got some business to attend to before then. Thanks anyway.'

He walked off before the man could stop him again, crossing the street and wishing he wasn't so conspicuously alone. He had better leave. He could catch a train or bus, stop off at some small, isolated place, and send out the recall signal for the ship to drop down and pick him up. Staying, while it could be exciting, could also embroil him to a dangerous extent and he didn't want to be reprimanded for immature behaviour.

It was while passing through some back

streets that he first learned he was being followed.

At first it didn't register, he had become so used to the lack of contact from the people around him and, when it did, he could hardly believe it. Someone was following him but, that someone wasn't a native of this planet! He halted, keening his mind for maximum reception, and, despite the nullifying effect of the planetary field, he could catch the emissions of another mind. The man, whoever he was, had halted too and was watching Gort with an almost gloating eagerness. Obviously he didn't suspect that Gort was other than what he appeared and, very obviously, he wasn't a Guardian.

But whoever and whatever he was he shouldn't have been here at all.

Slowly Gort continued walking, part of his mind taking care of his progress while the other, greater part, attempted to solve the mystery. Behind him he could sense that the man was coming nearer and, as he approached, his mental pattern became clearer. Gort cursed the peculiarities of this planet that prevented him from using his talents, the mental impression was fogged and blurred to an incredible extent and all he could catch was a sense of hate, of fury, and an overriding, almost sickening sense of hunger.

Gort activated his force-field just as the sear-blade lashed towards the back of his neck.

For a moment there was a struggle as energy combated energy. Sparks showered from the edge of the blade then it grew hot and began to smoke. The man, apparently half-dazed from the transmitted shock, dropped the weapon as Gort swung towards him. He recoiled, his eyes reflecting his hate and, as Gort moved closer he snatched at one of the buttons on his jacket.

'Turn it off!' Gort radiated the command with the full strength of his mind and, at the same time, grabbed at the figure before him. For a moment the two fields strained in conflict then, as that of the Guardian, more powerful and with greater efficiency began to override that of the other, Gort repeated his command.

'Turn it off, you fool! Quick!'

The answer was a blast of hate followed by a quick surge of fear. Confused impressions radiated towards him then, as Gort released his hold and stepped back, smoke and fire seemed to burst from the figure. For a moment he stood, limned in flame, then, as the overloaded protective field collapsed, he slumped and dissolved in smoking ruin.

Slowly Gort stooped and picked up the useless sear-blade.

★   ★   ★

Even in the early hours the railway terminal was fairly busy and Gort felt quite safe as he sat in the waiting room and waited for the night to pass. He was glad of the security because he had a lot to think about and, the more he thought about it, the nastier it appeared.

Of course, in a way, it had been inevitable. Someone, sometime was sure to stumble on the planet, drop down for a quick look, then try to make something from what they had found. The important thing was that they had managed to do it without registering on the detector screens of the moon-based Guardians. That was serious but, even more serious, was the trail of suspicion which the visitors were leaving behind them.

Gort sighed as he tried to collate his thoughts. Normally it would have been easy. As a Guardian he was a telepath and as a telepath he was automatically a Guardian but things, on this world, weren't normal. Telepathy was non-existent here. Trying to read the minds of the natives was like trying to read the thoughts of a steel ball. It couldn't be done. Whether that was due to the unique planetary field, or whether the very barriers behind which the natives lived affected his faculties, Gort didn't know, but the fact remained that, unless a broadcaster was right next to him, his ability was useless.

And there was more than just the one.

He relaxed and closed his eyes in pretended sleep as a policeman, suspicion clear in his expression, walked down the rows of seats. Gort had taken the precaution of buying a ticket for a train leaving shortly after dawn and he had a good reason for being where he was. He felt the presence of the officer as he halted and stared at him then, apparently satisfied by the slip of pasteboard Gort had stuck in his hat-brim, moved on.

The mental impressions he had received from the dying man had betrayed the presence of others similar to himself. Four others to be exact. And there was something about a ship, a rendezvous, and a time. The whole had been coloured with an overwhelming rage and a bitter self-blame at the loss of a wager. Recalling it made Gort feel mentally unclean.

Visitors from Outside would naturally be equipped with protective force-fields similar to, but usually less powerful than, the one he himself was wearing. Such fields always radiated and that radiation could be picked up by the proper detectors. Unfortunately he didn't have a proper detector and neither did he have the facilities for making one. Even if he had it would have been almost impossible for him to locate, hunt down, and render helpless four separated wearers of protective force-field jackets. The city was too big for that and, without his telepathic ability, Gort was suffering under a tremendous handicap.

He was like a man who owned a car, he could travel faster than any horse — until he lost his car.

He opened his eyes as a man sat down beside him.

'Sorry.' The man was fat, middle-aged, and obviously frightened. 'I didn't mean to wake you.'

'You didn't.' Gort felt that conversation would allay suspicion. The policeman was still patrolling the waiting room. 'Waiting for a train?'

'Yeah and it can't come too soon for me.' The fat man dabbed at his sweating face. 'I'm getting out of here while I'm safe. You heard the latest?'

'No?'

'That killer's been at work again. Five more people murdered and all found without heads.' He shuddered. 'That makes a total of eight, nine if you count the copper, and they still haven't got him.

It just goes to show you how good the police are.'

'They'll catch him.' Gort didn't think so but it seemed the right thing to say. 'Any clues?'

'They've found some of the heads. A boy picked up a suitcase and the damn thing was filled with them. What sort of man would go round doing a thing like that?'

Gort could tell him but he didn't think that the information would help.

'The police are going crazy,' continued the fat man. 'They've shot two men by mistake already and the jails are full of suspects.' He twisted his mouth as though he wanted to spit. 'A hell of a lot of good that's doing. The killer just keeps collecting more heads. They say that they know who he is though.'

'They do?'

'Yeah. A man name of Jones. He killed the cop in his hotel room. They're supposed to have seen him and shot him, but either they're lying or they were using water pistols. You can't tell me that a man can keep on running with bullets inside of him.' He lapsed into silence and glowered at the approaching figure of the police-man.

Gort waited until he had passed then rose to his feet. The pattern was getting clearer and he cursed himself for not having seen it before. Mason had given him the clue, and, aside from that, he should have suspected the use of a sear-blade when he had looked at the original corpse. But it had been so abrupt, so savage, that he had lost control of his reactions. He knew that it could never happen again, death, no matter how ugly, had lost its power to affect him, but he would have preferred to obtain his education the normal way. What had confused him was the fact that, to him, a sear-blade was a normal weapon. He had forgotten that here they were unknown.

Somehow he had to stop the inter-lopers.

7

San Luchin was enjoying himself. He crouched in the dark angle of the building and watched the bobbing lights of his pursuers as they hesitantly came towards him. The sight almost made him betray himself just to see whether or not they would repeat their useless attempts to kill him but, as his foot struck the suitcase by his side, he resisted the temptation.

The main thing now was to secure the safety of his trophies.

He had collected with the eye of a connoisseur rather than for sheer quantity. He had been clever too, far cleverer than those other fools who had taken trophies without regard as to time or circumstance. Aside from his latest acquisition, a female with a peculiar shade of red in its long, shoulder-length hair, he had been most circumspect.

Now, as he stared towards the lightening sky, he knew that it was time for him to retreat to his hiding place.

He had found one, a dingy, smelly, dirty lodging down in the poorer quarters of the city. A place where, as he suspected, his stolen money would grant him the few hours grace he needed until it was time to leave for the rendezvous. He waited until the bobbing lights were almost upon him then, his protective screen fully activated, he darted with deceptive speed from where he crouched.

A man shouted behind him. Guns roared in the confined space between the buildings and lead whined as it ricocheted from his force-field. Twenty seconds and he was around a selected corner. A door stood before him, it was locked but it opened as he fused the primitive mechanism. Through the building, his cat-eyes equally at home in the dark as the light, down a stair and up another, a second door and back onto the streets again with the entire block between him and his pursuers.

Again he repeated the manoeuvre, smiling with self-satisfaction at having planned the escape routes so well. To be hunted by things which, though they couldn't hurt him, yet betrayed the glimmerings of intelligence, was, to San Luchin, almost as good as the actual taking of a trophy itself. Mentally he decided to give Heltin a bonus for his services in finding this planet. He would return, of course, the next time armed with greater knowledge of local conditions. The mistake this time had lain in lack of preparation. They should have a base camp, somewhere the hunters could rest and plan their sport, a central location from which the hunters could strike out in distant areas and so be able to operate alone. Working with other hunters was never the same as lone sport. They tended to be too eager, too unthinking of the full consequences of their haste. Rivalry seemed to upset their judgment.

They became greedy.

★ ★ ★

It was after dawn when San Luchin reached his hiding place. The blowzy woman who let him in betrayed no surprise at the sight of his suitcase. To her he was a top-story man working the city under cover of darkness and, naturally, the suitcase was to contain his loot. All that mattered to her was that he paid well and caused no trouble. The pay she had taken in advance, the trouble she hoped would never come but, if it did, she wasn't totally helpless.

She locked the door after him and jerked her thumb towards the back room.

'Want anything to eat?'

'No thank you.' San Luchin was only eager to inspect his trophies but he couldn't tell her that. Instead he stared at her lined face, mentally visualising it on the wall of his trophy-room. It would do and, even if he chose to discard it, it would count for purposes of the wager.

The woman snuffled and wiped her nose.

'See anything of the killer?' If it was a joke it didn't sound like one. 'I've been listening to the radio and TV, seems to me the city's all upset.' She stared shrewdly at her lodger. 'It's a wonder you didn't get stopped.'

'I did.' The smile was awkward but he

managed it. 'Twice. But that was before . . . ' He closed one eye and hefted the suitcase.

'A good haul, eh?' Interest lightened her features. 'Let's have a look.' She misunderstood his hesitation. 'You can trust me, hell, I'm square, you can ask any of the boys. Maybe I can steer you onto a good fence if the stuff's right.' She reached towards the suitcase. 'Let's have a look.'

He let her touch the handle, enjoying the mental image of what she would do if she saw the contents then, as she fumbled with the catch, he reluctantly moved it from her reach.

'Sorry, but this is private.' He looked towards the back room from where had come the sounds of muttered conversation. 'Anyone in there?'

'A couple of the boys.' If she felt anger at what had just happened she didn't show it. 'Playing cards and killing a bottle. You want in?'

San Luchin shook his head and climbed the rickety stairs to his filthy room. He felt soiled when he looked at it but that couldn't be helped. Personal discomfort was one of the pleasures of the hunt. Not that it mattered, he was impatient to check his trophies for possible damage and, more important, eager to see that he had a representative collection. The time of rendezvous was getting close and he would have little time for other than a hasty hunt for the purpose of winning the wager. That he would win it he had no doubt, he knew his own capabilities.

Locking the door he set the suitcase on the bed and, opening it, lost himself in the pleasure of what it contained.

Time passed and it began to grow warm. It grew more than warm, it grew hot and, as he loosened his jacket, he felt the first impact of danger.

Too late!

Energy writhed around him, the trapped energy of his protective force-field, normally controlled and safe but now breaking loose. Desperately he tore at his smouldering garments then, as the safety margin was reached and passed, he turned into a literal living flame.

It lasted a split second then, with a

gush of released energy, he disrupted, the burning components of his clothing setting fires springing from the rotten woodwork and soiled bedclothes.

Within minutes the room was a raging inferno in which nothing living, or recognisable, could exist.

* * *

Gort thought that he had been rather clever. He looked around at the littered components on the bench and listened, not without guilt, to the muffled sounds coming from a deep cupboard. The sounds were caused by the owner and sole employee of the radio repair shop now bound and helpless after admitting his first customer. Gort had paralysed him, put him out of the way, locked the shop and set to work.

Now, several hours, later, he smiled with quiet pride at what he had made.

It was something that would have caused nothing but derision from the base techs, but it was the best he had been able to do. Knowledge, no matter how advanced is useless without tools and technology. Gort had the knowledge but he had had to build from hopelessly inefficient materials. That he had succeeded at all was something near to a miracle.

On a thick base he had assembled a mass of tubes, wires, altered resistances, adapted transistors, unrecognisable condensers, and a circuit which would have appalled the most knowledgeable mechanic in the business. It was a broadcasting unit of a very special kind designed to do one job and one job only. It would radiate energy which would set up hysterisis in a force-field and amplify it beyond normal tolerance.

He hoped.

Taking off his jacket he picked at a seam and, with exaggerated care, removed a thin, lustrous wire. He set it carefully aside on an insulated table and took a second and a third wire from the jacket. Then, having robbed his own force-field of its power source, he stripped and, carefully folding the clothes put them into a metal box. From the outside of the box he ran wires to the ground, then, finally satisfied, he returned to his wires.

Delicately he attached them to his hook-up, taking care that one should not touch the other, fastening them with insulated tools and working with a slow, careful sureness unknown to any but an expert. When he had finished he was trembling with reaction from strain. He waited a moment, checked the hook-up and, turning his back to the bench, closed a switch.

Light blazed from behind him as the power flowed from the wires into the circuit, was transmitted on a special frequency, and surged over the city. Opposite him, the ground-wires on the metal box containing his clothes glowed red, white began to slump, then faded to black again. The light died and, when he turned, the semi-molten mess on the bench defied recognition.

Dressed again Gort considered his next move. The unit he had built had worked and he knew that every force-field in the city other than his own had dissolved into fuming energy. The visitors whoever they were, would logically have been wearing those fields so, again logically, they had ceased to exist.

All that remained now was the ship.

The rendezvous, Gort knew, was set for tonight. The location was somewhere near or in the city, but just where he didn't know. Normally that wouldn't have mattered. His own detectors, though weak, would have been able to pick up the colossal radiation from any ship. But, if the ship was screened to avoid Guardian detection then it was certain to be able to avoid his own.

Frowning, he sat on the edge of the bench to consider. The dying mind of the visitor had visualised a stretch of ground bounded at one end by a poorly lit road, and Gort felt that it should be familiar. Within his skull the efficient mechanism of his mind began to correlate data and, when he finally slid off the bench, he was smiling.

He reached for the telephone on the counter and, after looking in the directory, rang a number.

'Police? I want to speak to Captain

Mason. That's right, Mason. Who's speaking? Holden. Gort Holden. That's right.'

He waited while the wires hummed.

'Mason? Holden here. I want you to tell me something.' Gort smiled at the noises coming from the instrument. 'Never mind where I am. I'm sorry about your wallet but I'll send it back to you. You can replace the money from that which you took off me. Now listen. That witness of yours, did he say that he'd seen me running towards some waste ground?' Gort frowned at the instrument. 'Please don't waste time. I know that you can probably trace this call but that doesn't matter. Did he? He did? Thanks, that's all I want to know. See you there tonight.' Gort went to hang up then let the receiver hang from its cord. They would be tracing his call and he didn't want to stop them. Someone had to free the irate owner of the shop.

8

He spent the afternoon and evening in a cinema, enjoying the sheer primitiveness of the reproduction medium and marvelling again at the inventive genius of these terribly handicapped people. It was dark when he stepped out onto the street and already people, scared of the mysterious 'killer' were hurrying home. An alley gave him all the concealment he needed and, beneath his touch, his force-field shielded gravity and sent him rising like a balloon. To steer himself towards the scene of the first crime was simple and, as he hovered in the shielding darkness, he grinned down at the shapes of lurking figures below.

Mason had the place surrounded.

After that there was nothing to do but wait. He didn't know the exact time of the rendezvous, only that it was for tonight, but he guessed that it would be around midnight or a little later. Actually it was two hours past midnight and he almost missed the ship altogether.

A rush of air warned him, that and a slight occlusion of his marker-points. Gently he lowered himself towards the invisible bulk until, as he penetrated the outer screens, he saw the scarred hull of the ship itself.

He was standing outside when Heltin opened the air lock.

'San Luchin?' The explorer stared outside. 'Where are you?'

Gort moved a step closer.

'San Luchin? Hurry up, will you, I want to get away from here.' He cursed monotonously as Gort didn't move. 'What's the matter? You hurt or something?' Impulsively he jumped from the air lock. 'I . . . '

Gort caught him as he fell, paralysed and helpless. Quickly he carried him back into the ship and, when Heltin recovered consciousness, he stared up into the disguised features of the Guardian.

'What goes on? Who are you?' Heltin climbed to his feet. 'Where are the people I brought here?'

'How many did you bring?' Gort used mental communication and the fact that he did so seemed to shock Heltin into an awareness of his position. He sagged and almost fell and when he had finally straightened his features were a peculiar greenish colour.

'The Guardians!'

'That's right. Well?'

'I'm just a pilot,' babbled the hapless man. 'I'm working on charter. All I know is that I dropped San Luchin with four of his friends here three revolutions ago.' He swallowed. 'You know about them?'

'What did you bring them here to do?'

'I don't know.' It was useless and Heltin knew it. To lie to the Guardians, or to any telepath was a waste of time. He turned to the attack. 'Well, what of it? So I've broken a few Regs, no great crime in that, is there?'

'Enough to earn you quite a period of immolation.' Gort was deliberately casual. 'You knew that San Luchin and his friends were hunters. You knew that they came here to collect trophies. You knew just what that meant to the inhabitants of this planet. You've not only broken quarantine but you've broken the Prime Ethic. I'd guess that you've earned permanent immolation.'

'No I haven't!' Heltin seemed about to collapse. 'These things aren't human. You know they're not. How could I have broken the Prime Ethic when I haven't killed or caused the death of a human being.' He looked triumphantly at Gort. 'You know that I speak the truth, you damn mind-leeches should be able to know that, and you know that all I've done is to bust quarantine.'

He was right. Technically the inhabitants of this planet weren't human and so Heltin hadn't been guilty of breaking the Prime Ethic. That was reserved for races who obeyed the one great requirement of the galactic federation. No member of any one race must ever kill a member of that race. It was the dividing line between human and non-human, men and monsters and, unfortunately, the inhabitants of Earth were still in the monster stage.

'You can't touch me,' sneered Heltin. 'So I get a few periods immolation, so what? Get on with it, Guardian, let's get it over with.'

Gort nodded, his mind busy with strange concepts. Heltin was guilty but, because of a technicality, he was going to get away with it. Unless . . .

Gort stepped forward and felt the slight body before him. No protective clothing. He jerked his hand towards the air lock.

'Outside.'

'What? Say, what are you up to. You can't do this to me.'

'Get outside or I'll throw you out at two diameters. Quick now!' He used the power of his mind and Heltin obeyed as he had to obey. Gort stood at the open air lock and threw Mason's wallet towards the shivering man. 'Right. Now walk to that road, drop that wallet, and come back here on the run.'

It was murder and yet, in a way, it wasn't. The Guardians had strong powers and were permitted to use their discretion. If Heltin returned he would be taken to the moon base to stand his trial. If he didn't . . .

The watching policemen had waited

hours and must have been getting tired but they woke up at the sight of a strange figure coming from nowhere. Heltin ignored the first challenge, he took fright at the second, he began to run at the third. The roar of many weapons blasted his body to a shapeless pulp.

Later, when well on his way to the moon base, Gort had time to assess his vacation. He had got out of a difficult situation without revealing his extra-terrestrial origin. He had stopped and punished the menace of an unauthorised visitation to a quarantined planet. He had provided a suitable suspect for the mysterious 'killer' and so had made Mason happy. He had taken charge of the ship, which had slipped past the detector screens and so would make Rhubens happy too. Promotion would be inevitable and Gort smiled as he thought about it.

Not such a bad vacation after all.

ETHICAL ASSASSIN

He was smooth and neat with liquid brown eyes, hair trimmed to clean perfection and clothes that were a quiet advertisement in good taste. He rested gloved hands on the edge of the desk and looked at Merrick.

'You realize just what you are asking me to do?'

'Certainly.' Merrick tried hard to be casual. 'I want you to kill a man.'

'Assassination isn't cheap. Why don't you call him out?'

'I'm not interested in legal dueling. I just want the man dead.'

'And if you called him out you might only hurt him — or he might hurt you.' The man nodded. 'He might even kill you. Is that what you're afraid of?'

'That's my business.'

'It could be mine,' said the assassin. 'Who is the man?'

'An engineer. Name of Blade. He

shares an apartment over in the seventh sector, 456, tenth level.' Merrick scowled as he thought of the man. 'There will probably be a woman with him.'

'His wife?'

'Yes.'

'Your ex-wife?'

'Perhaps.'

'I see.' The man looked at the tips of his gloved fingers. 'Are you quite certain that you want me to kill this man? Murder isn't nice and assassination is worse. If you hate the man so much then why don't you call him out? Fight him fairly with or without lethal weapons. You would get far more satisfaction by venting your rage personally.'

'I want him dead.'

'You understand that, once I accept this assignment, the man is, in effect, dead. That you are wholly responsible for his death and are guilty of illegal murder?'

'Never mind the legality of it. I understood that you would take care of the matter for me. I didn't ask for a sermon or a résumé of what I could or couldn't do. Do you want the job or don't you?'

'It is a matter of ethics,' said the man coldly. 'A human life is a precious thing — to the one who owns it. You may be in a passing rage, an emotional storm, which has confused your judgment. Later, you may be the first to regret what you have done.'

'An ethical assassin,' sneered Merrick. 'Will you accept the job or do I have to find someone else?'

'Have you twenty thousand credits?'

'Twenty thousand!' Merrick stared his incredulity. 'For a simple thing like squeezing a trigger?'

'For killing a man. Well?'

'I'll give you ten.'

'Twenty.'

'I haven't got twenty thousand. All I could raise is ten, and that's double what I expected to have to pay. What you ask is ridiculous.'

'You could call him out for the price of a videophone call,' reminded the assassin.

'No.' Merrick swallowed at the thought of physical violence. 'I can't do that.' He looked pleadingly at his visitor. 'Take ten thousand and kill him for me. Please.'

'You really hate him, don't you?'

'Yes. Will you take the ten?'

'I'll take it.' The man rose as Merrick counted out the money and stood, his liquid eyes enigmatic as he stared at his employer. 'It still isn't too late to call the whole thing off, you know.'

'I want the man dead.' Merrick licked his lips with gross anticipation. 'When?'

'That's my business,' said the assassin curtly. He walked towards the door, still smooth, still calm, leaving Merrick standing beside his desk.

He didn't offer to shake hands.

★   ★   ★

John Blade stood at the transparency and stared at the shimmering surface of the outer wall. Beyond that barrier the soil glowed with a faint blue radiation, grim reminder of what misapplied science had done to the major part of the world, but within the barrier clustered lights shone from terraced buildings and the scurrying dots of distant people showed that life within the city was carrying on as usual.

He turned as the door clicked open and a woman entered the apartment.

'Leena!' He stepped towards her. 'You look tired.'

'I am tired.' Wearily she slumped into a chair. 'Are they still in bed?'

'Yes.' He kept his voice low as he stared towards the bedroom door. 'They aren't due for going on-shift for another two hours. You're late, darling.'

'I know. I had some things to clear up, and one of the girls in the factory turned nasty. I had to call her out.'

'Hurt?'

'Not much. I chose padded clubs and gave her a few bruises.' She winced. 'I collected a few myself, but I taught the cheeky bitch to mind her manners.' She looked towards the closed door. 'I wonder if they'll be late or whether they'll get up early? I'm tired!'

'They'll be on time.' He sat down beside her and took her hand between his own. 'Any regrets?'

'At leaving Merrick?' She smiled and shook her head. 'Of course not. Oh, I miss the privacy of a single apartment, the privilege of being able to lie in bed and all the little luxuries of the Upper-Bracket Group, but I don't miss Merrick.' She squeezed John's hand. 'I wasn't sorry to cancel the marriage and sign a contract with you. Even if we do have to share an apartment with two other couples and only see each other for a few hours a day. It's worth it, John, and, perhaps, if we're very lucky, we might even be permitted to have a child.'

'Perhaps.' He didn't sound too hopeful. 'I shouldn't count on it, though, Leena. The city is near the breaking point as it is.'

'There's always room for one more,' she said, sleepily. 'And a baby is such a tiny thing.'

'But it grows,' he reminded gently. 'It grows awfully fast.'

'And that was the trouble. Babies grew and became men and women who, in turn, had babies. So the population grew and, when you tried to squeeze half a million people into a city designed to hold no more than half that number, things began to happen. Things like the sharing of living space with other couples, each working a different shift. Things like the total relaxation of all unnecessary laws and the resultant dueling code with its quick, summary justice and release of emotions. Things like easy marriage and easy divorce, radiation-induced sterility and rigorous control of birth. Things like the professional assassins.

'I'm worried, John.' Leena sat upright on the hard couch and rubbed the sleep from her eyes. 'I don't trust Merrick. Are you sure that he hasn't called you out?'

'Positive.'

'Then he's up to something.'

'What can he be up to?'

He smiled down at her, ruffling her hair. 'After all, why should he be upset? You were perfectly within your rights in divorcing him and marrying me. Merrick isn't a fool. He will accept the inevitable and, if he thinks that I've wronged him, then he can always demand a duel.'

'No, John. Merrick's a coward. He knows that in a duel he'd stand a chance of being hurt.' She gripped his arm with surprising strength. 'John! Suppose that he should hire an assassin?'

'Now you're being ridiculous, Leena. Assassins cost the Earth and Merrick likes money more than he dislikes me. Anyway, where would he find one?'

'He'd find one,' she said. 'Money can do a lot, John, and Merrick has money.' She gnawed at her lower lip, her face strained with worry.

'I didn't live with Merrick for five years for nothing, John. I know the way his mind works. He regarded me as a possession and hates you for taking what he believed to be his. He's going to want revenge. He's too much of a coward to call you out himself, but there's nothing to stop him hiring an assassin to do his dirty work for him.'

'Please.' He tried to soothe her and at the same time cover his own fear. In a duel a man stood an even chance of killing or being killed. Against a normal murderer a man still stood a chance for illegal murder was still punishable with death. But against an assassin a man stood no chance at all. It could happen any time, anywhere. A stab from a poisoned needle, a shot in the dark, a club swung from some hidden nook. The killer could be anyone, anywhere — the girl standing on the corner, the man asking for a match, the old woman who wanted help to cross the street.

'We don't even know that there are such people as assassins,' he said, slowly. 'Have you ever spoken to one? Hired one? You know that you haven't. They're just a rumor like the one about the outer wall failing or the land becoming useful again. Stop worrying about what doesn't exist.'

'You're wrong, John,' she insisted. 'Rumors must start somewhere and they usually start in truth. Merrick is rich and money can buy anything. Even you could hire an assassin if you wanted to badly enough. You could pass the word in a club, meet an in-between and, finally, you'd get your assassin. I've lived in the Upper-Bracket Group, John, and I know.'

'Maybe.' He looked up as the bedroom door clicked and a couple, their eyes heavy with sleep, entered the lounge. 'Good, they're early. Let's go to bed.'

He had almost to carry her to the still-warm couch.

★ ★ ★

The charge was formal, cold and utterly final.

'David Merrick?'

'Yes.'

'You are charged with illegal murder. Do you admit the charge?'

'No.' Merrick sweated a little as he stared at the two men who had entered his office. 'In fact I don't know what you're talking about.'

'Are you going to make this hard for us, Merrick?' One of the men, a slight, stoop-shouldered oldster, sighed as he looked at the papers in his hand. 'You hired an assassin to kill a man, a John Blade, now married to your ex-wife. You insisted on the execution of the crime despite all warnings. Will you admit this?'

'Certainly not! I . . . '

'Call Henson,' interrupted the oldster. 'This is a waste of time.'

Henson was the smooth, liquid-eyed man Merrick had seen before. He didn't smile in recognition, look guilty, upset or afraid. He stared at Merrick and nodded.

'This is the man.'

'Of course.' The oldster looked at Merrick. 'Do you still deny the charge?'

'This is fantastic! You're accusing me of hiring this man to assassinate someone. I deny it.'

'We have the serial numbers of the notes you gave him, the record of the conversation you had with him, and we even have the testimony of those you contacted to arrange the hire.' The old man put away his papers. 'And, of course, we have the evidence of the supposed assassin himself.'

'I don't understand.' Merrick sagged in his chair. 'Is Blade dead?'

'Of course not.'

'Then how can I possibly be guilty of illegal murder?' Merrick stared wildly at the three men. The old man, calm, a little impatient, seeming as if he had done all this a thousand times before. Henson, smooth and dignified, and yet betraying a trace of contempt. The third man, who had said nothing and who now leaned carelessly against the wall with his hand in his pocket.

'I warned you,' said Henson, coldly.

'I warned you more than once that, after I left this room, you were guilty of illegal murder. You accepted that and forced me to agree to kill a man for you. That makes you guilty.'

'But . . . ' Merrick gripped the arms of his chair. 'I don't understand. You say that Blade isn't dead and yet you say that I'm guilty. If I'm guilty then why isn't the assassin? Isn't he under arrest, too?'

'Why should he be? Henson never, at any time, had any intention of killing Blade. Only you had that.' The old man softened at the expression on Merrick's face. 'Can't you understand? There are no assassins. The whole concept is a fabrication, a deliberate temptation to the unstable. In a way you could call it bait for potential murderers.' He gestured towards the city beyond the wall of the office.

'Out there are half a million people living in cramped conditions and working like ants merely in order to stay alive. Those conditions aren't natural, Merrick, and neurosis and psychosis are so common as to be normal. That is why we have permitted dueling. Venting the emotions when aroused is the best catharsis there is, but assassination,' he shook his head, 'that is something entirely different.'

'Why? It's still murder.'

'Dueling isn't murder. Physical combat is face-to-face and as serious as the combatants wish to make it. It also serves a double purpose. Those who die by dueling are inherently of poor survival value. If they weren't then they wouldn't allow themselves to be killed in a duel. We can do without them, just as we can do without the diseased and the insane. You are insane, Merrick.'

'Ridiculous!'

'Is it?' The oldster glanced at the papers he had taken from his pocket. 'Cowardice and fear of physical assault. Primitive emotions with an unhealthy streak of possessive jealousy and inability to recognize the rights of others. Ungovernable rage and sadistic inclinations. Distorted values . . . ' He shrugged.

'Need we go on? You are a murderer and the rest is proved by your willingness to pay a ridiculously high sum to a man to do what you, yourself, dared not do.

The fact that your selected victim isn't dead means nothing. The intent is there and the intent is all we are concerned with.'

'It was a trap,' whispered Merrick, sickly. 'A dirty trap.'

'Exactly. We have to control the city somehow, and at the same time weed out the undesirable elements. One day we shall be able to leave the city and our people will have the task of re-populating the world. We want no dictators, cowards, killers, moral weaklings. We can do without primitive emotions, possessiveness, the inability to accept reality. Those things have done enough damage as it is.'

'The tout! The man I met at the club and who arranged the introduction!' Merrick stared accusingly at the oldster. 'If intent is as good as guilt, then isn't he guilty, too?'

'Like Henson, he is one of us, a member of the Psychological Bureau. You'd be surprised to know just how many agents we have scattered throughout the city, Merrick. They watch. They listen, and when they spot a man nearing the danger point, they are ready for him. Some we manage to save. Some are warned in time and recognize their need for treatment. Others, like you, are so far gone that they ignore all warning. Those we don't even try to save, though each gets his chance as you got yours. They are rotten stock, bad material, and the quicker we weed them out the better it is for those who are left.' The oldster sighed as he moved towards the door.

'You see, Merrick, no society can tolerate assassins; ours least of all. But the very fact that a man wants to hire one is, to us, a clear indication that he has become dangerously unbalanced. So we have assassins, ethical ones, not too hard to contact, and yet hard enough so as to give time for thought and reflection. They are, as you said, a trap. They offer the bait of easy murder and illegal death. But, of course, the only death they bring is to the one who employed them.' He nodded towards the third man, who stepped purposefully towards the desk.

'All right, Merrick. Let's go.'

Merrick didn't have to ask where.

WISHFUL THINKING

The room was a box twelve feet square, lined with tall green filing cabinets and centered by a desk. A desk lamp threw a sharp cone of brilliant light over the blotter, spilling onto the floor and illuminating the rest of the room with dim, unreal reflection. Two men sat at the desk, the smoke from the cigarettes coiling like a living thing in the close confines of the room.

'I don't like it.' John Evans, thin, gaunt, nervous, dragged at his cigarette and glanced at his watch. 'Thirty minutes now . . . You shouldn't have let him try it alone.'

'Carl insisted.' Sam Conway, falsely bland, sat and smoked and controlled his nerves with a lifetime of practice. He was a psychologist, a good one, and had long learned to master his emotions. John was a technician; a man who could dispense shock treatments, handle an electroencephalograph, perform electronic wizardry, and yet who was the slave of his own glandular reactions. He tensed as sound filtered into the room.

'Relax.' Sam had noticed the tension, recognized the cause, identified it and dismissed it. 'One of the patients having a bad time. Forget it.'

'I don't like it,' John repeated. 'If someone found us here they might start asking questions.'

'We're covered.' Sam crushed out his cigarette, hesitated, then lit another. 'There's nothing in the rules to say that we shouldn't get together in our off-time. If we want to talk shop and look up some case histories, then that's our business.' He chuckled. 'With the staff problem what it is no-one is going to jump on us for being enthusiastic about our work.'

'That depends,' said John dryly. 'We've been a little too enthusiastic. What with the mis-ordering of components, the misuse of machines and the misappropriation of funds we could be in real trouble.'

'Not if we succeed,' pointed out Sam evenly. 'And we have already succeeded far enough to justify what we've done. After Carl has finished his final series of tests we can publicize what we've done.'

John nodded, his logic telling him, as it always did, that his fears were unnecessary. As usual, logic yielded to pure emotion and he sat and smoked and sweated with anticipation of discovery.

Again sound filtered through into the room, distorted, almost unrecognizable, and yet, to an experienced ear, unmistakable.

'Number seven-twenty-three,' said Sam quietly. 'Paranoia.'

'Due for shock-treatment,' said John. 'She's already had insulin; now she's due for near-electrocution. When that doesn't work they'll do a lobotomy and release her as cured.' The way he said it left no doubt as to his opinion of the 'cure.'

'Not if Carl clears up the loose ends,' said Sam. He stared at his cigarette. 'Not ever again if what we are working on proves itself. No more drugs, electrocution, savage surgery. No more probing and questioning and blundering. Insanity will be cured the right and only way, by the patients themselves.'

'If Carl succeeds,' reminded John. He glanced at his watch again and, as he did so, his sleeve rode up his arm to reveal a thin, red line. Sam reached forward, gripped the wrist and stared at the mark.

'Still there?'

'Yes.' John looked at the mark. 'It's going fast. Another day and it will have vanished.' He drew back his arm. 'That'll teach me to control my imagination.' He returned to the subject foremost in his mind. 'Carl shouldn't be alone. One of us should have mentioned it to him as we did before. Why did you let him try it by himself?'

'I had no choice.' Sam shrugged, forcing himself to remain calm. 'I was delayed and Carl had locked himself in by the time I arrived. You know how he is, impatient as the devil, and he wanted to test the new circuit.'

'He's impatient,' admitted John. 'Too impatient, but he should have waited.'

'That's what I told him,' said Sam. 'He took no notice. Said that he'd run a test and join us here.'

'He's been alone for almost an hour,' said John. 'A test should last no more than a few minutes. Allowing for preliminaries he's still long overdue.' He crushed out his cigarette and rose to his feet. 'I'm going to join him.'

'And if the door is locked?'

'He'll open it or we'll force it open.'

They had to force it open. They did it carefully, mindful of janitors and repair men and the rest of the staff who might be curious as to why a laboratory door had been forced. And they didn't do it until it was obvious that Carl either didn't, or wouldn't, hear their calls and knocks. Sam produced a strip of steel, wedged it in the lock and levered back the latch. The door swung open. Sam stepped forward, switched on the lights and stared into the familiar room.

It was long, white-walled, grimly sterile and totally utilitarian. Cabinets of instruments and drugs lined the walls, hulking machines hunched over adjustable chairs and operating tables, and a complex switchboard hung against one wall. One corner of the long room was shielded by high screens, above which hung a single light. Sam stepped towards the screens and rolled them aside. Behind the screens rested a chair. In the chair . . .

'God!' Sam stepped back, his face ghastly. 'God!' he said again.

John didn't say anything; he was being violently ill.

★ ★ ★

Captain Kevin Stoner put down his book, tilted back his chair and stared up at the ceiling. He was a big, raw-boned man, his face seamed and with prominent cheek-bones, his lips thin, his short hair showing touches of gray. Like his body his hands were big, the palms broad and the knuckles scarred with old wounds. He had the physical equipment of a man of violent action, but now, as he leaned back and stared at the blank expanse of the ceiling, his eyes were those of a dreamer.

It was a trick he had, this relaxing and staring into nothingness. A trait that he had encouraged and developed during many years. Its practical use was attested by his rapid promotion from rookie cop to a captain in Homicide, for, at such times he was, in imagination, a different person in different circumstances. A murderer on the run, a killer lurking in darkness, a slayer who thought himself safe from discovery. It helped to be able to gain empathy with such a person — helped to put them where they belonged. But the trait had another, intensely personal aspect, too.

Now he was alone, bound, the walls of sweating stone, the air heavy with the stench of glowing charcoal and alive with the little, menacing sounds of boiling oil and touching metal. Feet shuffled towards him, soft, whispering as crude leather trod the reeking stone of the dungeon. They came nearer, nearer, and he tensed, straining mentally, against imaginative bonds, his heart pounding in his chest and the cold sweat of fearful anticipation oozing from his forehead. Desperately, he gritted his teeth, clenching his jaws against what was to come.

The door opened, Lieutenant Stanley entered the office, and the dream world vanished with the turning of the knob.

'What is it?' Kevin straightened, one hand picking up his book, the other opening a drawer in his desk. He moved smoothly, yet not so fast as to arouse suspicion. Stanley glanced at the book, caught a glimpse of the title and looked surprised.

'Historical stuff? Didn't know you went in for that sort of reading.'

'Some of it can be interesting.' Kevin poised the book in his hand. 'Ties up with the job, too. Did you know that in the old days they had the death penalty for most everything you can think of? Killing a deer, stealing, not paying taxes, any number of crimes. And they didn't burn their murderers, either.'

'No?' Stanley sat on the edge of the desk and helped himself to a cigarette from the captain's personal pack. He was thin, dressed in slouch hat and belted raincoat and looked just what he was, an underpaid, overworked detective who had long lost his illusions. He gestured towards the book. 'What did they do with them, hang them?'

'Sometimes.' Kevin tossed the book into the drawer, closed it, leant back. 'Mostly they used torture. Molten lead and boiling oil poured down the throat. Stretching on a rack, thumbscrews, hooks, boots which crushed the feet, and other things which crushed the skull.' He shuddered at recent memory. 'It makes you feel sick to think of what those poor devils must have suffered.'

'Different age, different ways,' said Stanley. He wasn't interested. 'Maybe they just didn't look at things the way we do.'

'Pain is pain, no matter what the age.' Kevin looked at the lieutenant. 'What did you want to see me about?'

'Call just came in from the city dump,' said Stanley. 'Old guy who acts as watchman phoned in to report the finding of a body.'

'Murder?' Kevin rose from his chair, his eyes alert.

'I guess so.' Stanley shrugged. 'I've sent off the wagon and the photogs. Doc Lancing is riding with the meat wagon. We won't know for sure until he gets through with his examination of it.'

'It's murder,' said Kevin decisively. He glared at the lieutenant. 'Why didn't you tell me this immediately?'

'Does it matter?' Stanley looked genuinely surprised. 'The stiff isn't going to get up and walk away.'

Kevin snorted and led the way from the office.

★   ★   ★

The city dump was a ten-acre stretch of rubbish half-filling the open maw of a worked out sand pit. Trucks from the city tipped their debris into the water, mingling broken bricks, builders' rubble and factory trash with the general garbage and junk collected by the city. A small bulldozer, red and yellow, squatted in silence close to a shack made of clapboard and corrugated iron. The shack looked as if a high wind would blow it back to the rubbish from which it had been built. A rusty stove pipe stuck up from one corner and a litter of old iron, salvaged timber, bricks and moldy rags surrounded it. A little way from the shack, close to the edge of the stagnant water, a cluster of men and vehicles gave life to a desolate scene.

'This is it,' said Stanley. He jerked open the door of the car, stepped to the ground and waited for Kevin to join him. Together, they moved towards the knot of men.

There wasn't much to see. Some rubbish had been moved and a man's shoe and trousered leg stuck towards the water. Kevin stared at it, glanced around to see if the photographers had recorded the scene, then gave orders for the rest of the body to be uncovered. As the uniformed police worked he singled out the watchman.

Old Joe McQuire looked as filthy as the rubbish dump, which he had made his home. His face was lined and seamed with dirt, his watering eyes reflected the stagnant water, his clothes had obviously been salvaged from the heaps of rags surrounding his hut. He wiped his mouth on the back of his hand and stared apprehensively at the captain.

'You found the body?'

'That's right.' Joe scuffed one broken shoe on the dirt. 'I was taking my usual walk and spotted a shoe. I went down and tried to collect it. When I found that there was a foot in it I near collapsed.' He pressed one dirty hand to his chest. 'I ain't as strong as I used to be and . . . '

'Skip it.' Kevin stared around him. 'You live in the shack?'

'That's right. The city hire me as watchman and I live on the job.'

'What are your duties?'

'I tell the drivers where to tip their loads and sign their papers if they have any. Mostly they haven't; it's a free tip. Then I try to keep the kids away from the water. Then, when Lem's here, I help him out.'

'The driver of the bulldozer,' said Stanley. 'He comes down twice a week and levels off, the dump. The drivers can't tip directly into the water for fear of getting bogged down.'

Kevin nodded. He had already grasped the picture. The old man, more scavenger than anything else, making a place for himself on the dump. His wages would be nominal, his presence enabling the city authorities to obey local ordinance, and he probably spent more time in salvaging rubbish for his own benefit than carrying out his duties.

'So you found the body while taking your usual walk,' said Kevin. 'Was it there yesterday?' The framing of the question was deliberate, the reaction as expected. 'All right,' said Stanley. 'Let's put it this way. Could it have been there yesterday?'

'No.'

'Sure about that?'

'I'm sure.' Joe rubbed the stubble on his chin. 'Lem was down yesterday and levelled off that area. I'm sending the trucks over to the far side now. Then they work back until Lem can level what they dumped.' He peered at Kevin. 'You don't think I had anything to do with it, do you?'

'Did you?'

'Hell, no! I told you, I was taking a walk and saw a shoe. I phoned in as soon as I saw something was wrong.' Joe rubbed his chin again. 'They were good shoes, too.' He seemed more upset about the loss of the shoes than that a man had died.

'The picture's clear,' said Stanley. 'This old coot makes sure that the trucks dump their rubbish so that he can take his pickings. When he's searched one lot he gets Lem to turn it over so as to make a second search.' He looked thoughtful. 'The body could have been dumped a couple of days ago under a load of rubbish. Or it could have been planted last night.' He glared at the old man. 'What happens at night? Is the place locked?'

'No.' Joe looked uncomfortable. 'The gate's busted. I've tried to keep it locked, but it's no good. A lot of couples come down here to smooch sometimes there's as many as half a dozen cars, and the kids swarm all over the dump. I do my best, but I can't be everywhere at once.'

'Where were you last night?' Kevin glanced towards the cluster of men, then back at the old watchman. 'Do you stay on the job all the time?'

'Mostly. Sometimes I take a walk into

town to see a movie or take a drink.' Joe looked furtive. 'You know how it is.'

'I can guess. So you wouldn't know whether a car drove in here on any one night or not.'

'Not for sure,' admitted the old man. 'Usually I hear them but pay no attention. They can't do any harm on the dump, and I'm too old to argue.'

'So much for the witness,' said Stanley. He seemed about to say more, but changed his mind as Doc Lancing came towards them. The doctor was no longer young, a veteran of two wars, and he had seen mayhem in many forms during his years as police surgeon. Now he looked white and sick.

'We've dug him out,' he said. 'Male, white, about forty and of medium heavy build.'

'How long dead?'

'About three days.' Lancing fumbled for a handkerchief and dabbed at his face and neck. Kevin looked at him with mounting impatience.

'All right,' he said, 'You know what I want. How did he die?'

'I'm not sure,' said Lancing. He put away his handkerchief. 'I'll make out a full report after the autopsy.'

'Poison?' Stanley asked the obvious question.

'Maybe. I can't be sure as yet, but I don't think so.' Lancing swallowed. 'All I can be sure about is that the victim suffered agonizing torture.'

'Torture?'

'That's what I said, and I meant it literally. The man, as a man, is almost unrecognizable.'

He wasn't exaggerating.

★　★　★

Director Hammond was a plump, jovial-seeming man who took pains to appear more like a prosperous man of business than the chief of the mental hospital that he was. In a way he was right to do so. Running a hospital, any hospital, required a shrewd talent for squeezing donations from people who first had to be persuaded that charity was a good investment. And Homedale, despite what he said, was not a good investment. Not, that is, in the restoration of a semblance of sanity to the mentally deranged without immediate financial return was compared to fat dividends paid regularly for money invested in gilt-edged shares.

But he tried. He tried because the initial drive that had led him first to study medicine, then psychiatry, had not yet been smothered by economic necessity. So he became more and more the beggar and less and less the man of science and, somehow, he managed to keep the hospital barely solvent.

'You see, Mrs. Cauldwell,' he said, and smiled as he said it. 'We each of us have a duty to the unfortunate. They come to us, the rich, the poor, the mentally ill, and we give them the best we have so that they may, once again, take their places in society.' Mrs. Cauldwell nodded. She was a fat woman, too fat, with a chin that kept beauticians happy, and a skin that defied cosmetics to appear youthful. She sat in Hammond's office and let her shrewd little eyes survey the luxurious appointments.

And they were luxurious. Hammond was no fool and knew his psychology. He knew that poverty repels and wealth attracts. So he had squandered needed money on satin-smooth panels, thick carpets, silver accessories on his walnut desk, expensive prints on his walls. The office reeked of money, of luxury, of comfort. It was a snare to garner more of the same.

'I'd like to help,' admitted Mrs. Cauldwell. 'I think that charity is one of the highest virtues, but . . . '

Her hesitation was obvious and Hammond sighed as he prostituted his art. The woman was willing to spend, willing to make a fat donation, but first she wanted him to convince her that she was doing a fine thing, a great thing, a wonderful thing. Privately, he wished that he could tell her just what to do with her money. Instead, he told her what she wanted to hear.

He piled it on. Words cost nothing, and her money was more important to him than his pride. He saved the most powerful argument until last.

'Naturally, any donation you should make to the hospital can be set against your income tax.' His smile was pure man-of-the-world. 'In that case a large donation would only cost you a fraction of its face value. It would mean a lot to us, little to you, but of course, that would not be mentioned in the publicity.'

She nodded, her eyes thoughtful and, watching her, Hammond had a moment of intense revulsion. He knew her type, knew it too well. She was the sort of woman, wealthy, jaded, who was willing to spend money for the opportunity of talking dirt to a man under the guise of psychological treatment. Her interest in the hospital was a fad, an opportunity to acquire a thrill but, as long as she paid for it, Hammond was willing to accommodate her. He rose to his feet.

'Would you like to see the wards? I would be happy to guide you over the hospital.' She agreed, as he knew she would, and together they left the soft comfort of the office for the bleak sterility of the hospital proper.

It was, in a way, a trip into hell.

The hospital was crowded, the staff overworked, the routine reduced to one of inhuman efficiency. Hammond led the way down a narrow corridor lined with, doors, each door fitted with a panel of toughened glass.

'Padded cells, 'he explained. 'For the most violent cases.'

'Violent?' She craned her short neck and peered through the glass. 'This one seems quiet enough.'

'They have their cycles of emotional activity,' said Hammond. 'Sometimes they just sit and withdraw into themselves, at others they will burst into unmanageable rages, and always we have to guard against the possibility of suicide.'

He continued the tour.

'This is the day room. Here we allow the milder patients to mingle and talk. Conversation amongst themselves is a form of therapy.'

'They look normal enough,' said Mrs. Cauldwell. She seemed disappointed.

'They are unpredictable, not violent, you understand, but maladjusted.' Hammond didn't even try to explain the various mental illnesses that made life a burden to each and every patient. He opened other doors. 'Occupational therapy, weaving, basket-making, painting, handicrafts, things like that' He gestured to the equipment clustered in the room. 'Many of the items made by the patients are of great artistic beauty.'

'Then why don't you sell them?' Mrs. Cauldwell sniffed as she asked the question.

'We do,' said Hammond quietly. He led the way towards the far wing of the hospital. 'Perhaps you would like to see the laboratory.'

'The laboratory?' She seemed disappointed.

'We call it that,' said Hammond. He didn't look at the woman. 'A better name would be the operating theatre.'

She smiled.

John Evans was working behind the screen when they entered. He straightened, his thin cheeks paling, then forced himself to smile as Hammond introduced the woman.

'Mrs. Cauldwell is very interested in

our treatments,' said the director. 'Would you show her some of our equipment?'

'Certainly.' John had been through all this before and knew what to do. He led the way to the operating table. 'This is where we give electric shock treatment,' he explained. 'Sometimes a high voltage charge can ease the inner conflict of a patient with beneficial results. The charge is quite high, almost equal to that of the electric chair, and it is applied through electrodes attached to the temples.'

'I see.' The woman reached forward and fingered the electrodes. 'Does it hurt?'

'Not really. The shock is of short duration and stuns the higher centers of the brain.' John was careless of his terminology, knowing that she would accept anything he said. 'If shock-treatment doesn't work, then we have recourse to outright surgery. You have heard of lobotomy?'

'Vaguely. Something to do with the brain, isn't it?'

'Yes. We insert a thin probe into the forepart of the brain and slash the tissues. The theory is that, if we can't fix it, we can destroy it.' John caught himself at Hammond's expression. 'The technique has proved most helpful in stubborn cases but, naturally, we try everything else first.'

'Why?' Mrs. Cauldwell frowned. 'If lobotomy is so successful, then why not just do it to all of them and save time?'

'The expense is prohibitive,' said Hammond smoothly, before John could speak. 'Lobotomy is a delicate operation.' He glanced around the laboratory. 'Where is Carl?'

'Gone.'

'Gone?' Hammond didn't pursue the subject. Instead, he smiled at the woman as he led the way towards the screened corner. 'I think this machine would interest you, Mrs. Cauldwell.'

'What is it?'

'An electroencephalograph, a machine which measures the electrical, emissions of the brain and records them in the form of a graph.' Hammond picked up a discarded recording. 'See? Those jagged lines are such a recording. With this machine we can diagnose the presence of brain tumors with almost a hundred per cent, efficiency. We can also distinguish between normal and abnormal mentalities with a fair degree of success.'

'Interesting,' said the woman.

'Very.' Hammond smiled at her as if struck by a sudden thought. 'Would you like to make a recording? It would be a pleasant souvenir of your visit.' His smile widened at her hesitation. 'It doesn't hurt. You won't feel anything but the light pressure of the cap on your head. John.' He gestured towards the technician. 'Take a recording of Mrs. Cauldwell.'

He stepped back and stood watching as Evans sat the woman in the chair, calmed her fears, adjusted the electrodes and turned to his recording drums. At first Hammond watched the woman, smiling with inward contempt; then, as his eyes strayed over the equipment, he frowned in thought.

The electroencephalograph looked different to when he had last seen it. There were more accessories, more banks of equipment; the entire machine looked far more complex than he remembered.

Hammond hadn't stepped inside the laboratory for a long time and hadn't inspected the equipment since it had been installed. Memory, he knew, could play strange tricks, but even his memory couldn't be so far out as to forget the cumbersome helmet made of glinting alloy, the writhing wires and hooded components humped next to the chair. Such things just didn't belong to the normal operation of the machine.

He smiled again as John released the woman and handed her a torn-off strip of paper. Hammond stared at it, recognized the typical pathological pattern, and smiled as he folded it and handed it back to Mrs. Cauldwell.

'A perfectly normal pattern. No trace of brain tumor or any aberration. I only wish that my own pattern showed so much stability.'

'You mean there's nothing wrong with me?' Her disappointment was obvious.

'Nothing organic,' assured Hammond. 'You are suffering from an unresolved inner conflict and your graph shows sign of tremendous nervous strain, but you are

131

far from being mentally unstable.' He sighed as he escorted her towards the door. 'It is only when we apply the fruits of modern science that we realize just what burdens many people undertake to carry. If I were to give my professional opinion I would say that you sleep badly, worry constantly, and feel a sense of insecurity. All this stems from the fact that you have never been properly understood. You are in conflict with yourself and those about you. The conflict is on the subconscious level, of course, and . . .'

His voice died away as he led her from the laboratory, along the corridor and up to the office and the final obtaining of her check.

★ ★ ★

The autopsy report read like something compiled from the files of the Inquisition. Kevin Stoner flipped the pages for the dozenth time, trying to make sense from what he read and, as before, yielded in disgust.

'Grim.' Stanley had his own copy of the report. He threw it onto the desk, produced cigarettes, lit one without offering the package to the captain. Stanley, like most men who live just beyond their income, practiced small economies. 'What do you make of it?'

'Someone didn't like the victim,' said Kevin dryly. He opened the report and looked at the typing. 'Lancing says that he's never seen such multiple injuries. Listen to this: interior of mouth and throat burned as if by boiling water; joints strained as if by deliberate tension; skin bearing numerous contusions, cuts and abrasions; large areas showing signs tantamount to burning; back and chest criss-crossed with marks of scourging with what must have been a loaded thong; internal injuries coincide with bruising on skin caused probably by impact with a blunt instrument.' Kevin glanced at Stanley. 'And that's not all. According to the report the man is a mess in every sense of the word. Death was caused by internal hemorrhage and shock. No signs of poison, though there are traces of other drugs, none unduly harmful. Death took place approximately sixty hours ago.'

'It fits,' said Stanley. 'Say they dumped the body soon after death. It was covered with rubbish and left. Next morning the dump-trucks covered it even deeper, but the day after the bulldozer came and leveled off the heap. The watchman went on the prowl to see what he could find and spotted the victim this morning.' Stanley nodded as if satisfied at his own deductions. 'It was pure luck that the body was found at all. One more day and it would have been buried real deep.'

'Luck,' said Kevin, and frowned. 'The boys get anything?'

'No. They've been the rounds but, as far as they can learn, no one's missing. I've had photographs made and circulated them to the missing persons bureau, the Salvation Army and some of the agencies. They may help.'

'I doubt it.' Kevin blew smoke at the ceiling, stared at it, then looked at the lieutenant. 'Done anything with the fingerprints?'

'Sure. I've wired copies to the central records, but we can't rely on them. They won't help unless he's done time, worked at a government plant, been in the armed forces or is an immigrant. But if he was an honest man who kept himself to himself, his prints will be just another set for the files.'

'Honest?' Kevin shrugged. 'I doubt it. Someone must have hated the victim pretty badly. Those injuries were done before death, remember. Now, who would want to kidnap a harmless, honest man and literally torture him to death? To me it looks like a vengeance killing, a gang job. Maybe he was a squealer. A welsher or a double-crosser.'

Stanley nodded.

'Could be,' he agreed. 'Maybe it wasn't even a local job.'

'It was local, all right,' said Kevin decisively. 'No one other than a local would have known about the dump.'

'They took a chance at that,' said Stanley. 'If the watchman had caught them dumping the body they'd have been in trouble.'

'If he had caught them then we'd be short one watchman.' corrected Kevin. 'That man's killers were ruthless. They didn't stop at just shooting him or crushing his skull. They took their time about it, slowly torturing him to death and probably enjoying every moment of it.' He tilted back his chair and stared at the ceiling. 'It was a premeditated crime, obviously. They had everything to hand for the job and that meant preparation.'

'How do you make that out?'

'The injuries must have caused intense pain. He must have struggled and screamed and fought. So he was taken to a place where his screams wouldn't be heard, where his killers could take their time and work in peace.'

Stanley grunted, neither agreeing nor disagreeing with the captain's deductions. He reached for his copy of the report and leafed through it.

'Clothes don't help. Cheap shoes, cheap suit, cotton shirt, no underwear or socks and no hat, at least we didn't find one. No cleaning marks on the clothes — they looked new, and nothing in the pockets.'

'Did they fit?'

'No. The clothes were too big and the shoes too small. Why?'

'Just a thought.' Kevin straightened his chair. 'Let's attack it from the other direction. So far we've assumed that someone prepared everything they needed for the crime and then lured the victim into the trap. Suppose the crime took place where everything was to hand. Clothes, shoes, instruments of torture. A place where screams and movement wouldn't be suspect. Somewhere local where a man wouldn't immediately be missed.'

'A hospital.' Stanley was disillusioned, but he was a long way from being stupid. He thought about it and then shook his head. 'It doesn't make sense.'

'We'll see.' Kevin riffled the report. 'Get a check on this clothing, see if it matches with that given out in the charity wards. Check to see if any of the staff or if any patient is missing. Send the boys round to check the dentists; you know what to do.'

'I know,' said Stanley. He grunted as he rose to his feet. 'But I think the idea's crazy. Only a maniac would have done a thing like that to a man.'

'Yes,' said Kevin softly. 'I've thought of that, too.'

★ ★ ★

Sam Conway filled in the last of the files before him, stretched, reached for and lit a cigarette. His head ached a little from a long, hard day, and he thought of a hot bath, bed, and twelve hours uninterrupted sleep.

He knew he would be lucky to get six.

The door opened and John, seeming to be thinner and more gaunt than ever, entered the office. He closed the door behind him and leaned against it.

'Ready?'

'I'm ready.' Sam glanced at his watch, rose, crushed out his cigarette. 'Everything under control?'

'Hammond was in the lab today.' John opened the door and led the way outside. 'He had some old crow with him; after her money I expect, and he had me make an electroencephalogram of her.'

'So?'

'So he was suspicious. Hammond's no fool, and he knows what an electro-encephalograph should look like. I saw him studying the additions we've fitted to the machine.'

'Experimental work is permitted,' said Sam calmly. They had reached the laboratory and he produced keys, opened the door, locked it behind him. John fumbled for a switch and light streamed from the single bulb suspended over the screened corner. 'Will you be the subject or shall I?'

'You.' John was nervous. He stared down at the chair, the glistening helmet, the humped equipment. 'When I think of what happened to Carl I get scared. Suppose it happened again?'

'It can't,' said Sam. 'Not while there's someone to do the monitoring.' He sat in the chair, adjusted it to a position of maximum comfort, snapped electrodes on his wrists, ankles and throat, then reached up to swing down the helmet. 'I'll take it easy,' he said. 'Five minutes and then you cut the power. Cut it sooner if you see any violent physical reaction.'

'What shall I watch for?'

'My wrist.' Sam stared at his left arm. 'I'll imagine that I'm wearing a heavy fetter, have worn it for a long time; there should be some reaction if the feed-back is still too high.' He lowered the helmet over his head before John could argue and, with the fingers of his right hand, tripped the switch in the arm of the chair.

There was no sound, nothing to show that delicate currents were being amplified, filtered, fed back into a circuit that consisted, in part, of the brain itself.

Sam first tensed, then relaxed, then tensed again. It was a minor tensing, a pantograph reduction of his imagined movements, but his muscles jerked a trifle and his skin seemed to crawl.

John watched the left wrist.

Sam was, he knew, now immersed in a dream world in which his imagination was the sole barrier to his accomplishments. It was, in a way, a complete release from the hampering barriers of reality. What Sam imagined he would experience, peopling his world with creatures of his own imagination. He could commit murder in that dream world, be a king, a slave, anything he chose. It was better than drugs, better than sleep, better than any other stimulus that had to be applied through the senses. For this stimulation came from the subconscious itself, was caught, amplified, fed back in such strength that the vague imaginings became seeming reality. He was seeing, hearing, feeling the amplified stimulus of his own imagination.

The left wrist twitched. The skin began to redden, to show roughness, to display the ghosts of sores and callouses to be expected when rasped by a heavy iron fetter.

John cut the power.

'Three minutes,' he said, when Sam had swung back the helmet. 'The psychosomatic affinity is still too strong.'

'Damn!' Sam sat and rubbed his left wrist. Even as he rubbed the markings faded back to clear, healthy skin.

'We seem to be licked every way we try,' he said bitterly. 'Too weak a feedback and there is no result. Too strong and the imagined world has a direct bearing on the physical well-being.'

'Are we still using Carl's new circuit?'

'No, that was too strong. I put in a moderation, but it isn't much better.' He stared thoughtfully before him.

'We've got to keep trying, John. The machine, as it is, is too much like holding a tiger by the tail. We daren't release it and it's too good to forget. If we can only lick this problem of too great a psychosomatic affinity between the physical and the mental worlds we've got something that will revolutionize the treatment of the insane. In fact, it will be the only treatment necessary.'

John nodded. He had heard all this before. Take a patient, put him under the machine and let his subconscious work off all its frustrations and conflicts in the harmless world of dreams. Let a man kill his father and marry his mother, a daughter kill her mother and marry her father and so get rid of the Oedipus and Electra complexes with their attendant feelings of guilt and shame. Let natural hate vanish in vicarious murder, let thwarted desires have free rein, let the whole twisted mess of insanity and aberration free itself by satiating itself in the world of dreams. For when anything is permitted frustration cannot endure.

It was the dream for which Carl had died.

★   ★   ★

Hammond sat at his desk and looked at the two men before him as if he still couldn't believe what he saw. Kevin Stoner, impatient and tired, glanced at Stanley, then back at the director.

'Have you sent for them?'

'Yes.' Hammond reached out to an intercom, pressed a switch, spoke into the machine. 'Have Evans and Conway arrived yet?'

'Just arrived, sir.' The voice echoed from the speaker. 'Shall I send them in?'

'Immediately.' Hammond switched off and stared at the two men as they entered the office. He made introductions, his shrewd eyes not missing John's sudden pallor or Sam's instinctive tension. They sat down, fumbling for cigarettes to cover their nervousness, keyed and tense as they stared at the officers.

'I'll make this brief,' said Kevin. 'Yesterday, a dead man was found on the city dump. We now know who he was, Carl Mayhew, a resident doctor to this hospital.'

'Carl, dead?' Hammond glanced at Sam and John.

'How?'

'He was tortured to death,' said Kevin evenly. 'He was savagely murdered, stripped, dressed in cheap, give-away clothing and then buried in stinking rubbish. Someone, apparently, didn't like the late Mr. Mayhew one little bit.'

'Impossible!' Hammond was shocked. 'Carl was one of the most popular members of the staff. Who could have done such a thing?'

'That,' said Kevin quietly, 'is what I intend to find out.' He stared at Sam and John. 'I've already made certain inquiries. I know that the clothing he was found in came from this hospital; it matches that worn by your patients. I know that he was very intimate with Evans and Conway, and they were in the habit of working

144

together at all hours. Conway has a car. The night porter here reports that he saw two men carrying a bundle enter a car and drive off at the critical time. When he checked he found that Conway's car was missing. He looked for Conway but couldn't find him, and next morning the car was back in its usual place. So the porter forgot about it until I questioned him.' He looked at Sam, his face expressionless. 'Ready to talk?'

'I have nothing to say.'

'And you?' Kevin stared at John. 'Did you quarrel with Mayhew? Did you hate him so much that you took him and tortured him to death?' Kevin took the autopsy report from his pocket and began to read aloud. 'Burning on the inside of mouth and throat. Hot water, Evans? Did you ram a funnel into his mouth and empty a boiling kettle into it?' He glanced again at the report. 'Multiple contusions and internal injuries. Did you kick him, Evans? Jump on him while he was lying bound and helpless? Did you . . . '

It was pure psychology, the playing of a man's weakness against himself. And, listening to the even, coldly clinical voice, Sam had to admit that the captain knew what he was doing. He seemed to have a peculiar imagination when it came to pain. He dwelt on every detail, lingering on just how the victim must have felt and suffered. Had he been speaking of a stranger it would have been bad enough, but he was talking of a friend.

John did the only thing he could do. He broke.

'Stop it!' he shouted. 'Stop it I tell you!'

'Do you admit you killed Mayhew?'

'I didn't kill him. No one killed him. We hid the body, yes, but that was all.'

'Suicide?' Stanley shrugged as if now he had heard everything.

'Yes.' John was desperate for belief. 'He didn't kill himself deliberately, but he died just the same. He was testing the machine and we found him in the chair. It was horrible! Horrible!'

'Steady!' Sam knew that it was time for him to take over. He pressed John back into his chair. 'What Evans says is the truth. We were working on a new discovery and Carl insisted on testing it alone. It killed him.'

'How?'

'I'll have to put it in layman's language, but perhaps you can understand. We developed a machine to increase the dream-world. We call it that for want of a better name. What it does is simple. It amplifies the subconscious and overrides the external stimuli so that thought becomes apparent reality. If you think you see a tree then you actually see a tree. A temple, the same; an army, the same; imagination has no limits. The . . . '

He went on with the explanation, trying to put into simple words the technical jargon of his profession. He stressed the affinity between body and mind, the psychosomatic effects of concentrated thinking, drew poor analogies and stated unprovable cases. And returned always to the one point he had to drive home.

'The machine is fatal with its attraction. You forget the passage of time, the external world, everything. The subconscious takes command, and the subconscious has no censor. There should always be a monitor to watch for the physical reactions and cut the power if things go too far. But Carl was alone.'

'And?'

'And so he died. Remember that, what he imagined, to him was real. And the more he sank into the dream world, the greater the feedback from his sub-conscious became, and the more violent his physical response became to the accepted stimuli. And the subconscious has no cen-sor. It goes the whole way.'

'I begin to see what you are getting at,' said Hammond suddenly. 'Pain and the love of pain. Carl?'

'Yes. Carl was a masochist. He literally tortured himself to death.'

★   ★   ★

Kevin was not an unintelligent man. He had read widely and garnered knowledge from odd corners. He knew what a maso-chist was, a person who derived pleasure from personal pain, and, assuming the existence of the machine, his death was logical.

But he needed proof.

Hammond, too, was not unintelligent and already his mind had leapt ahead. This trouble would be cleared up. The machine, because it had been developed with Homedale money and Homedale staff, would belong to the hospital. It would prove a boon to the treatment of insanity, but it would be more than that. Such a machine would be in immediate demand in the world of entertainment. His money worries were over.

Sam noticed the director's expression, guessed what had caused it, and inwardly smiled. Hammond was in for a shock. He explained why as he led the way across the laboratory towards the screened corner.

'This machine is no toy. It is dangerous, it can harm and, as we have seen, it can kill. Most people are cursed with the death-wish and, under the influence of the machine, that buried desire to escape from worry and responsibility will take over. It would be safe to say that, in its present form, the machine would decimate the population overnight.'

He glanced at Kevin.

'Ready?'

'What do I have to do?'

'Just relax. Then think of something, anything, and your thoughts will become real to you. After a while you'll find that you no longer have conscious choice of what you experience. That will be when the subconscious takes over. You can, naturally, exercise some initial control, and that control may last for a little while. But eventually you will, consciously, take a back seat.' Sam chuckled. 'It's surprising how many people have the buried desire to hurt themselves. Most of us suffer from one form of guilt or another and, subconsciously, we are always trying to punish ourselves. That is why I doubt if this machine will ever be a commercial proposition. It strips the veneer from a man, and most people do everything they can to retain that veneer.'

He watched as John adjusted the chair, attached the electrodes and lowered the helmet. A switch clicked, Kevin tensed, relaxed, tensed again. Hammond looked towards Sam and John, then glanced at

Stanley. He was worried. The machine overrode every other consideration. Sam and John were guilty of attempting to hide a death and misuse of equipment, but all that could be forgotten if only they could prove their point.

But they had to prove that Carl had died by accident. The minutes passed, slow, dragging, then Stanley leaned forward, his face white.

'Turn it off!' he ordered. 'Turn it off!'

Kevin had received his proof.

He was a masochist, too.

LAWYER AT LARGE

1

The charge was the usual one of sabotage and the accused, a pale-faced manual worker with a low-grade I.Q. and a disproportional emotional index, didn't stand a chance.

Mark Engles, Attorney-at-Law, listened with growing pessimism as the prosecutor gave the evidence. It was pretty conclusive. Three separate recording machines had registered the fact that the accused had entered the supply room of the automation section with metal concealed on his person. The same machines had also recorded the fact that he had left without it. Metal had been found in the supply hopper and baking furnaces of the cake-making unit. The estimated damage was over twenty thousand credits not counting loss of production.

Mark's own case was a laugh. The prisoner had refused to testify beneath the lie-detector and was relying on an unsupported denial of the entire episode. Privately Mark thought that he was guilty and so did the Union of Associated Pastry Workers who had briefed him to go through the motions of defense. He rose as the prosecutor finished giving his evidence.

'Your Honor,' he nodded towards the Judge, 'the defense wishes to point out that the entire evidence of the prosecution is based on various recordings. I quote the case of Smith versus Lampry; 369/45/2092, in which false recordings were used to secure an unfair conviction.'

'Objection,' snapped the prosecution. 'The case cited was one based on home-recordings. Those offered as evidence in this case were taken from sealed and certified sources.'

'Objection sustained,' said the Judge impatiently. He glared at Mark. 'The Court is surprised that you should rest your defense on so flimsy a ground.'

'The accused,' said Mark desperately, 'is of low I.Q. I also have certified evidence as to his emotional instability. At the time of the supposed crime he had reached the nadir of his emotional cycle and was approaching the manic depressive stage. I submit to the Court that he was not wholly in control of his actions at that time.'

'You wish to plead Justification?' The Judge looked astonished.

'I wish to plead mitigation,' said Mark firmly. He didn't look towards his client's agonized expression. To hell with him. The best Mark could hope for now was a reduction of sentence and even at that he was taking a long chance. He scowled at the evaluator. With a human jury he might have been able to sweet-talk them into an acquittal but emotions meant less than nothing to the cybernetic evaluator. Momentarily he wished that human juries hadn't gone into the discard twenty years ago.

'I offer the evidence of mental instability and emotional maladjustment. The accused, a craftsman, has a fixed neurosis against the automation in the factory where he was employed. The fact that it could bake a better cake than he ever could played on his mind to an extent where he was not wholly responsible for his actions. While not denying the sabotage I wish to point out that it was motivated on an emotional, not logical, level.' Mark drew a deep breath. 'We wish to throw ourselves on the mercy of the Court.'

The rest was simply a matter of routine.

A clerk took the certified transcript of the prisoner's emotional cycle and fed the data into the evaluator. The prosecutor, knowing that he had already won the case, at first was generous and allowed mitigation, then made matters worse by proving that the accused had never baked a cake in his life. The Judge was impatient at the delay and blamed it all on Mark. Finally the evaluator hummed and printed out its findings.

'Guilty as charged,' read out the clerk. 'Allowable mitigation five per cent. Reason: accused should have reported sick with emotional instability. Failure to do so condones his offence.'

And that was that.

★   ★   ★

Mark didn't stay to hear the sentence. He knew what it would be — five years corrective training and psychological adjustment. The allowable mitigation was far too small to make any difference and sabotage of the automation factories was a crime rapidly growing in importance to vie with that of outright murder.

He scowled as he thought about it. Somehow he was always getting the sticky ones. Trying to defend a defenseless case was bad both from the viewpoint of his own self-confidence and his business reputation. He guessed that the Union had only given him the brief because their own retained lawyers wouldn't touch it. A couple more failures to his credit and no decent firm would allow him to do so much as arrange a transfer of property.

He was still scowling when he bumped into Gale Hardin.

Gale, was big, fat, overdressed in the newest synthetics and exuded a sickly, commercialized charm. Mark knew all this and, at the same time, knew that Gale never had to worry about unpaid bills, lost cases or the cases that didn't just arrive to be taken. He didn't like the man but then he didn't have to. All that was necessary was for him to pretend that he did. He replaced his scowl with a smile.

'Gale! Good to see you.'

'Hello, Mark. How did it go?'

'The case?' Mark looked surprised. 'Were you in court?'

'I dropped in for a few minutes. I was showing Riphan around, thought he might be interested you know, but we left before the verdict. Did you get an acquittal?'

'Guilty as charged,' said Mark bitterly. 'It was hopeless from the start. I even pleaded mitigation and only got a lousy five per cent. The Union will love me for that.'

'They should care.' Gale shrugged. 'You shouldn't have accepted their brief anyway. You'd have done better making a deal with the insurance company.'

'On the damages?' Mark frowned. 'I don't get it.'

'Simple. If you could have swung the verdict to total insanity the insurance company wouldn't have had to pay out on the factory damage claim. They could have pleaded non-co-operation. The factory medical staff would have had to take the blame for permitting an insane worker to remain in employment.'

'But he wasn't insane,' protested Mark. 'Anyway, would the insurance company have been interested?'

'Not officially, but they'd have sent you a present if you'd have made a deal with them. You could even have run the two, taken the Union brief and worked for the insurance people at the same time.'

'And the accused?'

'He got time, didn't he? What's the difference where he spends it? At that you'd have done him a favor, they tell me that the mental homes are a lot better than jail.'

'Sounds nice,' said Mark sarcastically. 'Unethical, of course, but what's the risk of losing my license against money in the bank?'

'That's right,' said Gale cheerfully. He hadn't noted the sarcasm. 'Ethics hasn't paid any bills yet that I know of.' He glanced at his wristwatch. 'Look, Mark,

I'm busy right now, but I may have something for you. You any good on partnership deals?'

'I passed in commercial law,' said Mark stiffly, then remembered to smile. 'Why?'

'May have a job for you. Will you be at your office this evening?'

'Yes.' Mark hadn't intended to be there but he was in no position to pass up the chance of employment. With the law schools turning out more lawyers than could possibly be used no one could. Gale nodded.

'I'll call you. Right?'

He was gone before Mark could answer.

2

Mark rented a half-share of an office down in the poorer section of the city. His co-sharer, a self-styled private investigator who apparently lived on hope and charity, was out and Mark was glad of it. He was in no mood to listen to long, involved stories of adulterous lovers or about the time when Sam had had to chase a runaway husband all the way to the Moon. That, apparently, was the high point of Sam's career in more senses than one, and he was never tired of repeating it to anyone willing to listen.

Kicking shut the door Mark picked up the few letters on the mat and crossed to his desk. The mail was still hand-delivered in this area and so was always received at least two days after posting. Not that it made any difference; bills, circulars and official notifications of court-sittings and changes in procedure didn't suffer from the delay. Throwing them into the waste chute

Mark sat down behind his desk and waited for the call that might never come.

Sam returned while he was still waiting. The private investigator was a small, wizened man with little shrewd eyes and a twisted ear that he consistently refused to have fixed by plastic surgery.

'Adds to the picture,' he explained. 'Gives me that air of toughness a private eye should have.' Secretly he wished that the damaged ear, which he had received during a fall when young, had been a scarred cheek or something more romantic. He nodded to Mark, and put a paper carton of coffee on the desk.

'Busy?'

'Hope to be.' Mark looked hopefully towards the coffee. Sam grinned and produced a couple of paper cups.

'I guessed that you'd be in. How did the case come out?'

'Rotten.' Mark sipped at the coffee Sam poured out for him. 'And you?'

'I've just been paid for a thing I did.' Sam didn't explain and Mark knew better than to ask him. A born romantic Sam hated to be tied to reality. He had probably earned some money hustling packing cases or carrying luggage at the spaceport, but he would have died rather than admit it. He looked on the mat as if in search of a letter.

'Any mail for me?'

'No.'

'You sure? I was expecting a cheque.'

'No mail,' repeated Mark tiredly. He had been through this before. 'What's the matter, can't you pay your half of the rent again?'

'Well,' Sam almost had the grace to blush, 'you know how it is, Mark. Big things are moving but the money's slow. I'll pay it back, honest I will.' Mark grunted.

'I paid a month's rent out of my retainer. But it's the last time, Sam. You pay next month's rent or we break up this happy partnership.'

'Thanks,' said Sam cheerfully. He poured more coffee and they sat for a while in silence as they drank it. The videophone hummed as Mark finished his cup and, dropping the empty container, he reached for the remote and switched on. A girl's face simpered at him from the screen.

'Mr. Mark Engles?'

'Speaking.' Mark moved so that the scanners could pick up his image. 'You want me?'

'Oh, Mark,' she simpered. 'Of course I want you. I want you to be with me on the most romantic trip ever devised. Just think of it, dear, you and I together on the Tycho Express. Dancing to the soft strains of Gibbon's Glowlights in the Earthlight Bar. Cuddling in . . . '

'A lousy commercial,' said Sam as Mark switched off. 'What'll they think of next?' He frowned at the dimming screen. 'Not bad though. Direct contact and plenty of appeal. The spacelines must be getting desperate to try anything as raw as that.'

'Raw is right,' snapped Mark. He was irritable at the reaction. He had expected Gale to call, not some painted female trying to kid him into buying a trip to the Moon.

'The starlines have got them worried.' Sam was still thinking of the commercial. 'No one wants to go to the Moon or the planets now. Why should they? Nothing to see up there and a lot of expense to see it. Now that the Federation's contacted us they'll be running trips to the stars soon. Lots to see and do, no need to wear suits and no need to be cramped up for weeks at a time.' He sighed. 'We're living in a great age, Mark. A great age.'

'If you've got the money,' conceded the lawyer. 'Me, I'd rather have the old days.' He smiled at Sam's shocked expression. 'All right, so I'm against progress. But I'm a lawyer and lawyers always are. Back in the last century we'd have both been rich. I'd have bought a snug practice and spent happy weeks in court arguing with men instead of machines. Corporation and criminal law paid well in those days. They didn't have evaluators then, nor all these recording machines, nor automation. A man got into trouble and, guilty or innocent, a lawyer got him out. Look at the fortunes some of those old-timers died with! I tell you, Sam, they had it easy in those days.'

'Maybe,' said Sam. He didn't seem convinced.

'There's no 'maybe' about it,' insisted Mark. 'I've read the old cases and I know. They had plenty of time then and a case might take days to settle. Then there were little tricks and things that slowed down the trial no end. Now what've we got? Machines! A machine in the jury box. A human judge, sure, but he's there just to check admissible evidence and to pass sentences. Everything's got to be facts, trimmed, isolated, fed into the evaluator. Emotion's got nothing to do with it and money even less. Either a man's guilty or he's not guilty. A man's got to be a logician now if he wants to be a lawyer.' He pointed a finger at the private investigator. 'Know what my old professor used to say? He said that unless a man is a good chess player he should give up all idea of entering the law as a profession. He's got to be able to think three moves ahead and base his case on unassailable logic. That's the only way he can hope to win.'

'Tough,' admitted the little man. 'But maybe it's got its good points. I mean, suppose I was accused of something, murder, say, there wouldn't be much chance of my getting immolated for it if I hadn't done it, would there?'

'No, but that isn't the point. Murder cases never did pay off. It was the litigation which made the old-timers rich. Partnerships and property settlements, wills and trivial things which ate up the cash and kept the lawyers on velvet.' Mark sighed as he thought about it.

'We'll get by,' said Sam encouragingly. 'It's just a question of getting to know the right people and stepping in at the right time. Now take a case I had once. I saw a couple kissing in a car. Nothing to it you say, but I felt differently. They didn't kiss like a married couple and I was curious. I followed the woman home and found out that she was married. Her husband . . . '

Mark sighed. Sam was off again and there would be no stopping him until he'd finished. In sheer self-defense Mark began to read a law-book on partnership law while the little man's voice droned in his ears.

It seemed to go on forever.

3

Senator Kingsman, the accredited representative of the state of Arizona, was a worried man. Despite that fact he managed to smile at his visitor and go through the customary details of hospitality and time-wasting maneuvers before he allowed his guest to get to the point. When he did he was brutally direct.

'Senator,' he snapped. 'You've got to do something about these aliens.'

'Do?' Kingsman managed to keep his expression bland. 'What can I do?'

'I don't know and I don't care but whatever it is you'd better do it soon.' Harland, president of Trans-Solar Spacelines didn't trouble to hide his impatience. 'Unless something's done soon we'll be out of business. Traffic, aside from the usual essentials, is down to a trickle. The space fleet is traveling with low rate payloads and the concessionaires are screaming for blood.' He paused. Your blood.'

'Mine?' The Senator looked shocked. 'Really, Harland how can they hold me responsible for the unfortunate fall-off in trade?'

'Because they voted you into power,' said Harland. 'Or rather we paid for the votes, which comes to the same thing.' He looked directly at Kingsman. 'You've had it easy so far Senator. Now's the time for you to start working for what we've done for you.'

'Please!' Kingsman knew that his study was private, he didn't even have an old-fashioned telephone so as to beat the wire-tappers, but some things shouldn't be talked about even in private. He made certain that the doors were locked, the electronic heterodyning barrier working as it should, and the windows shielded. Harland watched him make sure of his privacy with ill-concealed impatience.

'Satisfied?'

'You can never be too sure,' said Kingsman. 'Only the other day a Senator was arraigned for private deals inconsistent with his high calling. A snoop managed to focus a parabolic microphone on him while he was discussing a deal. I don't want that to happen to me.'

'It won't,' promised Harland. 'At least it won't as long as you play things our way.' He sat back in the chair, a heavy-set man with hooded eyes and a cruel mouth. 'Now, let's get to the point. We gave you the election because we wanted someone in a position to take care of our interests. The way things are you aren't doing that.'

'How can I? I can't make people travel on your spaceships. Anyway, you still have the monopoly of supplying the colonies with staple foods.'

'Bunk,' said Harland shortly. 'What staples? With their automation factories all they require is power and raw materials. Power they have in plenty — atomic power. Raw materials aside from trace elements and rare earths they have all around them.' He glowered at the Senator. 'You know what we are ferrying to Mars now? Vitamins! Two ship-loads and they have enough to last them for the rest of the century. The same to Venus. Tycho takes a little more but that's mostly luxury goods. It's getting to the point where we're making the trips for the fun of it.'

Harland fumbled in his pockets, produced a cigar case, selected one, bit off the end and lit it with an inlaid lighter.

'The most profitable commodity we can carry is the tourist trade. Men and women, boys and girls with a pocket full of credits and a yen to see the System. Nothing else we can carry pays as well.' He glared at Kingsman through a veil of smoke. 'Surprised? Why should you be? A tourist is ready made. He pays a hundred credits a kilo passage money. He's a two-way payload. He spends money on arrival and so our concessionaires are happy to pay us for their concessions. Add souvenirs, extra freight charges for overload, food and drink other than the basics consumed during the voyage. Add insurance premiums, personal recommendations and repeat trips and you've got a juicy slice of business.' He took the cigar from his mouth and scowled at the tip. 'We want to keep it.'

'Naturally,' said Kingsman. 'And you blame our visitors for the fall in trade?'

'Yes. They can offer more than we can. Their starships are bigger, smoother, more comfortable. But aside from that they offer what we can't. Trips to the stars. Who wants to look at the deserts of Mars when they can travel to another solar system? So people are saving up for when they can buy a berth on a starship.'

'That's silly,' protested Kingsman. 'The aliens aren't offering passage to anyone. All they've done so far is to land a trading and investigation commission. It may be years before they begin offering travel facilities.'

'And in the meantime we starve,' said Harland grimly. He looked at the Senator. 'Have you any suggestions?'

'No,' said Kingsman unhappily. He was beginning to wish that he'd never got mixed up with Harland. Still, if he hadn't then he would never have been elected and he liked his job. He liked it very much. Harland shrugged.

'Very well, then, let's examine the problem. How do you stand as regards the aliens?'

'I haven't thought much about it,' said

Kingsman cautiously. 'I've been waiting to see how things turn out.'

'Sitting on the fence, eh?' Harland nodded. 'Well, now is the time for you to get down and start fighting. What's the picture?'

'Well,' Kingsman was still uneasy at breaking government confidence. 'They want us to join their Federation and open our markets to trade and general business. The President is dithering. He hasn't had the final go-ahead from the World Council and yet he knows that if he does accept the rest will fall in line.'

'So he's sitting on the fence too? Why?' Harland shot the question as though it were a bullet from a gun. Kingsman swallowed.

'The aliens have the interstellar drive. We want it. The President hopes that they will give it to us in return for joining their Federation.'

'And will they?' Harland was eager. Kingsman shook his head.

'They say not. They say that we must pass a period of probation before we are given the knowledge to build our own star fleet. They remind us of the fact that the World Council is only fifty years old and that it only came into being because of war. They say . . . '

'To hell with what they say,' snapped Harland. 'The position is this. They won't give us the drive so we can't compete with them. At the same time they want us to join them so that they can skim our trade. That means they will soak up the tourist trade from Trans-Solar. That means we go out of business.'

'No it doesn't. You'll still have the government charter to supply and contact the colonies. You've got the mail contracts too.'

'We can do without them,' said Harland curtly. 'Anyway, what's to prevent the aliens from running their own interplanetary service? With the ships they have they could do it easily while waiting for an interstellar cargo. Trying to compete with them would be the same as a man on a raft trying to grab the trade from an ocean liner.' He dragged savagely at his cigar. 'Damn them! I've built up Trans-Solar from a couple of ferry rockets supplying the television station to what it is today. It's a good service and I'm proud of it and I don't want those aliens coming in and making us all feel small.' He looked at Kingsman. 'You've got to stop them.'

'How?'

'How do I know? Vote against them. Lobby against them. Line up the Conservationists and the fanatics, do some horse-trading and line up some opposition.' Harland grinned. 'You won't find it so hard. I'll get to work on television and the media. A few rumours and a whispering campaign should help things.' He grinned again. 'I want the choice of two things. Either they give us the drive so that we can enter into full competition with them, or they get to hell off Earth and stay off for good. Of the two I'd prefer the drive.'

'I doubt if you'll get that,' said Kingsman unhappily. He could see that his future wasn't going to be pleasant. Harland shrugged.

'Then get them kicked off of Earth. I don't care how it's done but it had better be done soon. Otherwise someone else will be warming your chair in the Senate and you'll be feeding an automatic for a living.'

Harland grinned through the smoke of his cigar.

4

Gale didn't videophone, he called in person. Sam was still talking, this time about a case he had worked on a long time ago, when the door swung open and the fat man entered the room. He stared about him as Mark, quick to seize an opportunity, silenced Sam with an expressive gesture and filled in the silence with smooth talk.

'I understand, Mr. Leman,' he said. 'I'll get to work on it right away. Ten tomorrow suit you?'

'Yes,' said Sam. He winked. 'Thank you Mr. Engles. I'll tell Fenman that you'll accept the case.' Fenman was the local numbers king. He ran a semi-legal racket depending on the winner guessing the total number of items produced by the automatics in the city. Gale waited until Sam had left the office, his broad-features expressionless. If he had caught the blatant falsity of the conversation he

179

made no sign of it. He sighed as he plumped into Sam's chair.

'My feet are killing me. Riphan wanted to see everything and he wanted to walk. Wouldn't have a drink handy, would you?'

'Sorry.' Mark didn't have to look. He knew that any liquor in the office would have been drunk by Sam long ago. Gale sighed again and slowly drew a flat bottle from his side pocket.

'I thought so, that's why I bought my own. Got any glasses?'

Mark hadn't but he salvaged the paper cups they had used to drink the coffee, rinsed them beneath the faucet, and stood them on the desk. Gale broke the seal and poured out a generous measure of whisky into each cup. He sipped, grinned, and sipped again.

'I needed that. Riphan doesn't understand why men should poison themselves for pleasure so I had to remain on the wagon while I was with him.' Gale emptied his cup and refilled it from the bottle. 'Busy, Mark?'

'So, so. I've something coming up tomorrow.'

'Fenman?'

'Maybe.'

Gale chuckled with a force that sent little quivers running over his fat. 'Don't kid me, Mark. You're broke and you know it. Fenman wouldn't touch a lawyer like you, anyway. He's too big.'

'So he's too big,' said Mark coldly. 'Is that what you came to tell me?'

'No.' Gale took his time drinking his second helping of Scotch.

'I mentioned a partnership, Mark. Remember?'

'I remember.'

'I want it fixed like this. My partner to share responsibility as well as profit. Can do?'

'A simple commercial contract would cover that,' said Mark. 'Each partner to be fully responsible for debts incurred by the other partner or partners within the business. Such responsibility to be the full extent of capital, income and possessions. Each partner to be fully responsible for any unethical or illegal conduct, other than criminal conduct, by any other partner or partners, each partner to share in any and all profits and capital possessions of the partnership according to previous agreement. Any such agreement does not, however, reduce the liability of any partner which shall always be equal to any other partner or partners.' Mark drew a deep breath. 'Still want it?'

'I think so. Why?'

'It's a dangerous business,' explained Mark. 'A partnership is all right with a well-established firm but to enter into one with an unknown is begging for trouble. He can ruin you before you know it. Better form a limited liability company. It's safer.'

'But not as binding,' said Gale shrewdly. 'I'll take my chance. When can you have the contract drawn up ready for signature?'

'Tomorrow morning. I'll have to get an authorized form from the court,' explained Mark quickly. 'I can be your witness, my licence permits me to administer the oath, but I can't do anything about the seal.'

Gale thought about it for a moment, then nodded. 'Okay. I guess tomorrow will have to do though I was hoping to get it finished tonight.'

'Makes no difference,' assured Mark. 'It won't be legal, unless deposited at court anyway.' He drew a scratch pad towards him.

'You might as well let me have the relevant information now. Name of company?'

'Interstellar Traders,' said Gale smugly. 'There'll just be the two partners, me and Riphan.'

'Riphan? The alien?' Mark looked dubious. 'That alters things.'

'Why?'

'There hasn't been a decision on their legal status yet. Until there is this partnership won't be valid.' Regretfully he put away the scratch pad. 'Sorry. Gale, it looks as though we can't do business.'

'Why not?' The fat man dabbed at his moist forehead. 'Don't kid me, Mark. I've sunk all I own into this thing and I'm in no mood for humor. Draw up that form and leave the rest to me.'

'It'll be a waste of time,' warned Mark. 'It won't be any more valid than if you entered into partnership with a sixteen year old. No court would uphold it. More, both of us would get into trouble, you for insisting and me for permitting.'

'Not if it isn't deposited at court,' said Gale shrewdly. He leaned forward across the desk. 'Look, Mark, I'll come clean. You know that I've been running around with Riphan, showing him the sights, getting friendly, all the rest of it. Well, I didn't do it because of my health. Riphan's a member of the trading commission and wants to get into business. He's got a warehouse of stuff ready for the markets and can arrange lots more. I managed to get in on the ground floor and that's where I want to stay. This partnership agreement will tie him up and put him where I want him. There!' Gale made an expressive motion with his thumb.

'You're playing with an H-bomb,' said Mark grimly. 'Riphan isn't a moron, he'll catch on for certain.'

'Riphan is an entrepreneur,' said Gale. 'Like me. He saw a chance to make a profit and took it. Why do you think he's been running around with me instead of staying with the rest of them at World Council Headquarters? That boy's smart. He wanted to feel out the market and get organized before anyone else has a chance. If I don't tie him down someone else will.'

'Not until he has legal status,' reminded Mark. Gale snorted his impatience.

'To hell with his status. Let me get him to sign that form and he'll believe that we are partners. As his partner I'll have access to his stuff. It's worth millions, Mark. Billions! It's the chance of a lifetime!'

Gale sweated with the thought of it and dabbed at his forehead again. His eye fell on the bottle and he drank straight from the neck.

'Listen, Mark, I've got it all worked out. You get the form and leave the date blank. We sign it and, if ever the aliens get legal status, you fill in the date and deposit it in the normal way.'

'No,' said Mark. He helped himself to the Scotch, the strong whisky burning his stomach and reminding him that he hadn't yet eaten. 'It wouldn't work. You're underestimating Riphan, Gale. He must be a pretty shrewd customer to even think of trading on a new planet. What makes you think he'll sign anything without advice?'

'I've thought of that.' Gale grinned at his own cleverness. 'I took him into court while your case was on. I did that for a reason, he now knows that you are an accredited member of the bar. You can show him your licence and he can check with the records or with anyone he pleases. We aren't trying to pull anything on him, Mark. All I want is to become his partner. The only thing we needn't tell him is that he has no legal status. Even if he knows that it needn't make any difference. Better still, in fact. That way he'll have to trade through someone who has got it. I just want that someone to be me.'

'Sounds reasonable,' admitted Mark. He took another drink of the whisky. To hell with worrying about ethics! He was hungry, his pockets were empty, and the spirit was going to his head. A man never got anywhere being honest. Let the suckers take care of themselves. Money in the bank was your only friend. He needed a new suit. He stared at Gale.

'What's in it for me?'

'That's the boy!' Gale grinned his relief. 'You'll do it?'

'Maybe. What's my cut?'

'A hundred down and a hundred more when the job is done.' He looked at Mark. 'What's the matter?'

'I can't see so good,' explained Mark. 'Those figures are too small.'

'All right,' sighed Gale. 'I need you, Mark, and I'm willing to pay. 'Five hundred cash for the job. Five hundred more for your signed contract to represent me at any time if and when I need a lawyer. Agreed?'

'Why you? Why not the firm?'

'Same thing, isn't it?' Gale winked. 'Be your age, Mark. Once you're in you might as well get in all the way. Call the second five hundred a retainer and you'll know what I mean.' He took a bulging wallet from his pocket and Mark felt quick regret that he had not asked for more. He took five hundred, letting the crisp fifty-credit notes crackle in his fingers, then put them away and wrote out the commitment. He held it out to the fat man.

'Here. Call me to any place, any time, and I'll come running.'

'Thanks.' Gale took the slip and stuffed it into his wallet. He corked the bottle and slipped it into his pocket.

He was grinning as he walked out of the office.

5

Senator Kingsman was going strong. He stood before the Senate, a commanding figure with his carefully whitened hair, his carefully massaged cheeks and his bland, innocent features. His voice, the only genuine thing about him, was just rough enough not to annoy and yet cultured enough to ensure respect. He was delivering a tirade aimed at the aliens, he was careful never to call them Lomians, and nothing was too bad for him to accuse them of.

'They came here,' he said, 'uninvited, unasked, uncalled for. They came in their ship and what do they do? They tell us, the inhabitants of this planet, that we are to join their Federation! They tell us, the owners of this world, what to do! Their audacity, ladies and gentlemen of the Senate, is paralleled only by their insufferable insolence in informing us that we are too backward, too primitive,

189

to be entrusted with the secrets of their science. And yet . . . ' Harland grunted and switched off the tri-di color screen. For a moment the figure of the Senator mouthed in silence, then, with a blur of washing color, he dissolved into pearly-gray nothingness.

'Nice repetition,' said Vernon. He lounged in his chair, his pale blue eyes almost closed and his flaxen hair falling over his forehead. 'Who wrote it?'

'Some professor from the Semantics Institute.' Harland didn't believe in letting his left hand know what his right was doing. 'How are you getting on with your part of the job?'

'Fair enough. I've got fifty people out on the whispering campaign. I've got another hundred spreading rumors. By this time tomorrow everyone will have heard that a chambermaid was attacked with dishonorable intent — and that she was bribed not to make a complaint. They will also have heard that three babies are missing and believed to have been stolen by the aliens. They are the rumors. The whispering campaign is that the aliens are trying to get our secrets without giving us any of theirs in return.'

'And your future programme?'

'After three days we release a further set of rumours,' said Vernon languidly. 'I've got some really good ones lined up from plague to destruction of the automatics and radiation danger from the engines of their ship. Have you fixed the schedule with the papers?'

'The reports will appear,' promised Harland. 'Have you found anyone ready to swear a complaint yet?'

'I've a couple lined up.'

'I want them more than lined up,' snapped Harland impatiently. 'I want them ready to move.'

'You'll get them.' Vernon didn't let the big man's impatience worry him. 'It isn't as easy as you make out. I've got to select people close to the aliens, women for preference though men will do in a pinch. It's no good them swearing out a complaint if the defense can prove that they were nowhere near the aliens at the time of the incident. Even your fancy conditioning so that they can fake lie-detector testimony won't help in that case.'

'I'm not concerned in getting a conviction,' said Harland coldly. 'All I want to do is to arouse a stink. The bigger the stink the better chance we'll have of getting them sent home with a flea in their ear.' He frowned down at his fingernails. 'I wish that I could think of some way to make them want to go of their own accord.'

'I can think of a way,' said Vernon. He smiled at Harland's expression. 'No I'm not telling you. For one thing you wouldn't stand for it and for another it's best for you not to know.'

'Then don't tell me,' said Harland quickly. He scowled out of the window to where a hundred foot sign advertised the beauties of the Earthlight Bar at Tycho. 'How is the advertising going?'

'Three complaints as to violation of privacy causing domestic crisis.' Vernon chuckled. 'Our direct contact advertising on the videophone made some wives think that their husbands were having an affair. The fools switched off too soon.'

He shrugged. 'A letter of explanation and apology together with a half-rate Tycho Express offer smoothed them out. No need to worry.'

'Better not try that again, anyway,' said Harland. 'I never did think much of it, undignified and the customer reaction may swing opposite to what we want.'

'I disagree,' said Vernon calmly.

'Perhaps, but we won't try it again.'

'No? Would you like me to tell your pilots how to operate their ships?' Vernon stared at the big man. 'You needn't answer. They know their job and I know mine. While I remain in charge of advertising we advertise in the way I think best.' He smiled. 'Now don't lose your temper, Harland. My schedule doesn't permit any alteration. What if we do arouse a little negative reaction? We haven't got any competition that I know of and they either ride with us or stay at home. And they won't want to stay at home.'

'And the aliens?'

'I'll settle the aliens.' Vernon relaxed, smoothing his flaxen hair. 'How far can I go on expenses?'

'As far as you like — if it does the job.' Harland smiled at the man in the chair. 'If it doesn't you'll be out filling in blast pits.'

He kept on smiling.

6

The videophone hummed and Mark switched on to reveal the taut face of an athletic-looking man.

'Brother,' said the man, 'are you lonely?' He gave a wink. 'Let me tell you about the girls on Venus. For . . . ' His face gaped and swirled as Mark cut the connection. Another lousy advertising stunt instead of a customer. He wondered savagely how they expected lawyers to live. He could go chasing ambulances, he supposed, but no, all that was taken care of by the Mutual Protection Agency with their resident lawyer at each hospital and morgue. Advertising was out, he'd tried that and lost money with only a flood of circulars and a single client who wanted him to take her case on a strict no-win, no-fee basis. The case had been hopeless and he'd had to refuse.

Thinking of cases made him remember Gale. He hadn't seen either the man or his alien friend since they had signed the partnership agreement several days ago. He wondered how the fat man was making out.

He looked up as the door opened and the object of his thoughts came bursting into the office.

Gale was sweating with the effort of moving quickly. He slammed a brief case onto the desk and slumped into a chair. He gasped, fought for breath, and pointed at the brief case.

'Hide it. Quick!'

'Why?' Mark didn't touch the case. He stared at the fat man until Gale managed to recover his breath and could talk like a human being.

'Take care of it for me, Mark.' Gale smiled with his mouth. 'It's private papers, some stuff I want you to take care of for me. Will you?'

'Take care of it? Sure, why not.' Mark lifted the brief case and stepped out of the office. Sam, coming towards him down the corridor, stared curiously at the brief case.

'I've seen that before,' he said. 'That fat character was carrying it.'

'That's right.' Mark gave him the case. 'Take care of it for me, will you? Hide it somewhere and let me know how to find it later.'

'Sure.' Sam took the case. 'Trouble?'

'I don't know yet.' Mark watched as the little man vanished down the corridor and then returned to his office. Gale had fully recovered and was lighting a cigarette. He offered the pack to Mark who took one, puffed it into life, then stared at Gale. 'Want to tell me?'

'It's Riphan.' Gale looked ugly. 'That lousy alien wants to revoke on our deal. I've given him a transcript of the laws appertaining to partnership agreements but he doesn't want to play. He said that he didn't know I was a crook and wants to call the whole thing out.'

'Why?'

'I pledged his credit,' explained Gale. 'As his partner I had advance information the way things were going.' He chuckled. 'At least that's what everyone thought. He found out about it and turned nasty. I grabbed my stuff and came straight here to warn you.'

'Warn me?' Mark looked blank. 'What about?'

'He's going to file a complaint with his commission. That means they'll take it to the Supreme Court. You said yourself that administering the oath on that partnership agreement was against the law. Yet you did it and collected a fee for the job. If Riphan complains you'll lose your license for sure.'

'No I won't.' Mark smiled at the fat man. 'I never deposited that contract. Once I destroy it there'll be no proof against me whatever. All I need to do is to deny the whole thing. No evidence no case. You should learn some law, Gale.'

'Should I?' The fat man sighed. 'I've got a surprise for you, Mark. You haven't got that contract, I have.' He looked apologetic. 'I thought it would be safer with me so I had one of my friends take it out of that tin box you call a safe.'

'Breaking and entering. That's a felony.'

'Not really. A man is entitled to his own property, Mark. Or would you like to explain to the court why you retained it in your possession?'

Mark felt a sudden chill. Gale was right, he was heading for serious trouble if the matter ever came to light. Malpractice was more than just frowned upon. It ranked with sabotage as a crime, and was treated accordingly. It didn't matter as to the degree of malpractice either, the evaluator took notice of big crime or little crime. It was only interested in crime. He looked up as the door swung open again and Riphan entered the office.

Mark had seen the alien before, all the world had seen one or the other of them, either on television or by personal contact, and the main feeling had been one of surprise that they differed so little from men. There were differences, of course, the head-crest, for one, the seven-fingered hands for another. They were a little taller than a man and had a blue tint to their skins. That and the slit-pupils of their eyes were the only obvious differences.

'I want my papers,' said Riphan without preamble. His English was almost too perfect. 'You stole them and I want them back.' He glanced around the office. 'Where are they?'

'I don't know what you're talking about,' said Gale coldly. He stared at Mark. 'Tell this blue-skin where he gets off. Tell him that any assets of a partnership are joint property. Tell him that.'

'I am not your partner,' said Riphan. 'I want my papers.'

'Well?' Gale remained staring at Mark. 'You're my lawyer. What are you waiting for?'

'Is this the call you paid for?'

'Yes.'

'Very well.' Mark sighed and turned towards the alien. 'What's all the trouble about?'

'This man has stolen some papers from me. They were not the property of the firm he tricked me into joining. Even if they were he has no right to them. The partnership was invalidated by his failure to disclose to me the fact that he was once accused of false representation.'

'I was acquitted,' said Gale.

'That does not matter. Under Lomian law a full declaration must be made before an accredited witness. This man,' the alien gestured towards Mark, 'is an accredited witness on this planet. You failed to make a full declaration. Therefore the contract is invalid. Incidentally I intend to make a complaint to my commission. This man has caused me much expense and inconvenience.'

'Wait a minute,' said Mark. Privately he cursed the fates for even having mixed him up in this business. 'Must you do that? Make a complaint, I mean. I assure you that we acted in good faith.'

'I do not doubt it,' said Riphan politely. 'You also seem to have been deluded by this man. However, as I wish to retain an unblemished business character. I have no choice. The failure to report a crime is equal to participating in one. May I have my papers now?'

'Look,' said Mark desperately. 'If I give you back the papers will you forget about making a complaint?' He ignored Gale's gesture of protest. 'Can't we make a deal, your papers for your, silence.' For a moment he thought that the alien would agree, then, reluctantly, Riphan shook his head.

'No. The papers aren't as important to me as my business reputation. If it was ever discovered that I had condoned a crime I would be accused, penalized, and banned from trading. I cannot risk that. I am sorry but I must report the entire incident to my commission.'

He moved towards the door.

'Hell,' said Gale. He rose to his feet and put one hand into his side pocket. 'Riphan!'

'Yes?'

Gale shot him with something he had taken from his pocket. Immediately he turned and threw it towards Mark. Instinctively the lawyer caught it and stared at a small pistol. He looked from the gun to where the alien had slumped in an untidy heap on the floor.

'He's dead,' he said stupidly. 'You killed him.'

'That's right,' said Gale. He was sweating but he forced a grin. 'What are you going to do about it?'

Numbly Mark reached towards the videophone.

7

The case was scheduled to be tried in three days' time. Because of the repercussions, the open-and-shut nature of the case, the obvious guilt and certainty of conviction, delay had been cut to a minimum. Politics too had something to do with it. The Lomians, shocked and horrified at the wanton destruction of one of their number, were demanding justice. The World Council, terrified that the newly contacted Federation would either take their own justice or, worse, refuse to maintain their contact, had slashed what little red tape there was to give priority to the trial.

Everything was over but the shouting.

Mark thought so and felt sick in his insides as he thought about it. Gale would be certain to bring everything out at the trial and Mark had an uneasy feeling that he wouldn't be a lawyer for much longer. Tiredly he punched the activating button as the videophone hummed and stared at the smooth face of a flaxen-haired man.

'Mr. Mark Engles?'

'Speaking.'

'My name is Vernon. You don't know me and have never seen me. I am interested in the case of Gale Hardin.'

'So?'

'So I suggest that you go and see him at once.'

'I can't. I don't want to. Even if I did want to he's held incommunicado.'

'True, but as his lawyer you have the right of access.'

'His lawyer!' Mark glared at the smooth face of his caller. 'What gave you that idea?'

'He did. Something about a signed promise to attend him whenever he called. He mentioned that a fee had been paid.'

'That call was taken care of when he shot the alien.'

'Was it?' Vernon shrugged. 'I understand differently. I understood that he still holds a certified form of yours.' He shrugged again. 'I know little of the law but isn't it considered to be unethical to accept a retainer and then refuse a case?'

'Not if the case is detrimental to the business reputation of the lawyer.'

'Was that specified?' Vernon smiled. 'Never mind. I'm sure that you can sort out all these little difficulties with Mr. Hardin. He's waiting for you, Mr. Engles. Goodbye.'

His face faded and Mark scowled at the blank screen. Vernon, whoever he was, had managed to deliver the threat beneath a seeming cloak of innocence. The certified form he had mentioned was that triple-damned partnership agreement. Gale was using it as a club to make Mark attend him in jail and, if Mark hoped to salvage anything from his career, he had to see the fat man.

★ ★ ★

It wasn't easy to locate the prisoner. Finally Mark ran him down in an out-of-town precinct and fumed impatiently while the officials tried to think of every excuse in the book to deny him access. They only yielded when he lost his temper.

'Look,' he snapped, 'Mr. Hardin has my written promise to attend him whenever he should call on my services. That makes me his accredited lawyer. If you refuse to let me see him I'll file a complaint at the Bar Commission. I'm not going to be penalized for unethical behavior because of you.'

They checked his claim against the property they had taken from the prisoner and found the signed slip. Mark took it, stuffed it into his pocket, and followed the turnkey into the consultation room. Gale grinned at him as he entered through a second door.

'Mark! It's good to see you.'

'Is it?' Mark sat down and glared at the fat man. 'Why did you send for me, Gale?'

'Isn't that obvious? You're about the only lawyer I can trust to represent me in court with the intention of securing an acquittal instead of throwing me to the wolves.' He held up his hand against Mark's protest. 'Now take it easy, Mark.

At least listen to what I have to say before you fly off the handle.' He stared around the room. 'Is it safe to talk?'

'Yes. These rooms are supposed to be inviolate. Anything said between us is on a confessional level. Even if they have wired the place they can't use what they hear as testimony for the prosecution. If they tried it we would win the case by default.' Mark shifted uncomfortably on the hard chair. 'What makes you think that I'll agree to represent you?'

'Because you've got no option,' said Gale coldly. He smiled at Mark's expression. 'Look at it from the prosecution angle if I should choose to talk. You and I were partners in a criminal enterprise, getting Riphan to sign that contract. You knew that you were breaking the law. Riphan found out about it and threatened to complain to his commission. That meant you would be accused of malpractice and penalized for it. To stop his mouth we had to kill Riphan. That makes you an equal partner in the killing because all acts stemming from an illegal association are deemed to

be the joint responsibility of that association. Right?'

'You wouldn't,' said Mark despairingly.
'You know damn well that I had nothing
to do with the murder.'

'No? Your fingerprints were found on
the gun. You were present at the scene
of the crime. You had a motive for killing
him and you were mixed up in the
swindle.' Gale grinned at Mark's expression. 'So it's a frame. So what? With the
way the World Council are feeling they'd
be only too glad to give me company on
the way to permanent immolation. It will
boost their credit with the aliens and give
them a couple of brain-unit cybernetic
controls. What have they got to lose?'

'I'll testify beneath the lie-detector.'

'And you'll have to confess your
criminal knowledge of the partnership
swindle.'

'All right,' said Mark grimly. 'So I lose
my license and get jailed for a few years,
that's better than immolation.'

'Sorry, Mark, but it isn't as easy as
that.' Gale looked at the tips of his
fingers. 'I'm in a jam and I need help to

get out of it. The only help I can trust is that of a man who is as deep in it as I am. That's you. I took the precaution of having a little conditioning done on me and, if you go under the lie-detector, then so will I.' He smiled at Mark. 'I will testify that we are equal partners in the killing and the machine will support my claim.'

'Conditioning? That's illegal.'

'Maybe it is, but that doesn't alter things.' Gale stared directly at the lawyer. 'My only chance to get an acquittal is to have a lawyer who is fighting as hard as he can to get it. No deals, no arrangements, no compromises. The only sort of man who will do that in the face of World Council pressure and public opinion is someone who has everything to gain and nothing to lose. In other words, Mark, if I get immolation then so do you. If I get acquitted then you're in the clear with a big reputation and a pocket-full of money.'

'An acquittal! But how?'

'That's up to you,' said Gale easily. 'You're a smart lawyer, Mark. Think about it for a while and maybe you'll get the idea. If you need any help call Central 234/543, you know who to ask for.' Gale rose to his feet. 'That's all, Mark. Just remember that whatever happens to me will happen to you too. See you in court.'

Mark nodded, waiting until the turnkey had come and removed the prisoner.

He wished that he could feel as confident as Gale seemed to be.

8

Central 234/543 brought the flaxen-haired man to the screen. Mark stared at him and tried to guess where Vernon fitted into the pattern. Conditioning took money, skill, and a practitioner who wasn't too particular about what he did. The penalties for illegal conditioning were severe and it took a lot of persuasion to override them. 'Mr. Engles!' Vernon smiled. 'I had expected you to contact me earlier. You saw Mr. Hardin?'

'I did,' said Mark grimly. 'Just where do you come in on all this, Vernon?'

'Does that matter?' Vernon kept on smiling. 'Let's just say that I'm interested in the case from a humanitarian point of view.'

'Humanitarian or financial?'

'Both. You need money?'

'I will do. How much can I spend?'

'That rather depends,' said Vernon thoughtfully. 'How much do you need?'

'Lots.'

'For personal reasons or for benefit of the case?'

'Benefit of the case.' Mark stared at the screen trying to see the background beyond the flaxen-haired man. All he could make out was a shapeless blur; Vernon had cut all lights except those essential to the scanners.

'If I may make a suggestion?' If Vernon had guessed why Mark had moved out of focus as he almost pressed his nose against the screen he made no sign of it. 'Suppose you tell me what you need and I'll foot the bills. Or, better still, just tell me what you need and I'll obtain it.' He hesitated 'On what grounds do you propose to base your defence?'

'That's my business,' said Mark curtly. Vernon shrugged.

'As you wish. But may I remind you that you cannot afford to make any mistakes? A man's life is in danger and perhaps it would be wise for you to discuss the case with someone else.'

'You said that you didn't know anything about the law,' reminded Mark.

'Anyway, I only called to find out how far I could go in the matter of expenses.'

'As far as you like. Just tell me what you need and I'll obtain for you.' Vernon smiled. 'Nothing illegal, of course.'

'Naturally,' said Mark sarcastically. 'Nothing like a little conditioning for example?' He cut off before Vernon could answer.

Sam came in while he was sat glaring at the screen. The little man looked seedier than ever and nursed a badly scratched face.

'I drew a bad one,' he explained to Mark. 'I figured I might scare up a little divorce evidence but the wife clawed me before I could put the proposition to her. Seems that she's known all along about her husband running around and doesn't care about it.' He looked thoughtful. 'Maybe she's cheating too? Perhaps her husband might be interested instead?'

'Maybe he'll break your jaw if you try it,' said Mark savagely, he was in no mood to listen to the tribulations of the little man. Sam shrugged.

'Maybe. Say, Mark, about that case you

gave me. I put it — '

'Don't tell me,' said Mark quickly. 'Just hold it until I ask for it.' He didn't explain that what he didn't know he couldn't tell. Once under the lie-detector a man had to tell the truth as he knew it and Mark had the feeling that, just possibly, the brief case might be important. He looked at the small man.

'Got a job for you, Sam,' he said curtly. 'Can you find out who and what a man named Vernon is? I don't know where he lives but his videophone number is Central 234/543. Get me all the information on him you can. Right?'

'Money work,' said Sam, 'or just as a favour?'

'Money work.'

'I'm on my way.'

Mark sighed as the little man left the office. No matter what Sam found out it didn't alter the main problem. He had to secure an acquittal for a man who had deliberately shot down an alien before witnesses with all the weight of public and political opinion against him. He was still brooding about it when the door opened and a tall, thin, haughty-faced man entered and stared distastefully about him.

'Mr. Engles?'

'That's me.' Mark glanced up and then leapt to his feet. He had only seen the visitor once before but every lawyer knew John Morgan, President of the Bar Commission, the one man whose single word could make or break a promising attorney. Hastily he dusted off a chair and placed it for his visitor.

'I'll come to the point, Mr. Engles,' said Morgan stiffly. 'I understand that you are shown as the lawyer defending Gale Hardin. Is that correct?'

'It is.'

'I realize, of course, that every man is entitled to be defended no matter what his crime. I do not blame you for accepting the brief However, as there is not the slightest possibility of you winning the case, and as the World Council are perturbed as to the possible repercussions in their dealings with the Lomians, I suggest that the sooner and cleaner the case is closed the better for all concerned.' He twitched one tufted eyebrow. 'You follow?'

'I think so,' said Mark. 'You want me to make a deal with the prosecution.'

'That will hardly be necessary,' said Morgan stiffly. He seemed to be upset by the hint of collusion. 'No, all that is necessary is for you to make your token defence, admit the crime, and appeal for mercy. The entire case should be over in an hour.' He glared at Mark. 'As you actually witnessed the murder you are liable to be called by the prosecution unless you can persuade your client to plead guilty.'

'Personal convenience should not condone unethical behaviour,' said Mark piously. He glanced around the bleak dinginess of the office. 'I had hoped that the case would give me some favourable publicity. I had intended to make it last at least two days.'

'A quick conclusion will be appreciated,' said Morgan. He rose to his feet. 'In fact I have an opening in my own firm for a young lawyer who can couple discretion with imagination.' He paused. 'On the other hand I should not wish to be in the shoes of anyone foolish enough to insist on beating his head against a wall. The case takes place in two days time, Mr. Engles. Need I say more?'

Mark shook his head.

9

The entire compliment of Lomians attended the opening of the trial. They sat in silent dignity while scanning lenses swung towards them and cameras clicked and whirred from all sides. With the Lomians came the representatives from the World Council, the Senate, the Bar Commission and everyone who could somehow, someway, gain admission. The Judge, a noted humanitarian, took his seat and the Court got down to business.

'Case Hardin versus the State,' droned the clerk into the recorder. 'Case number 765/784 circa 2113. Charge of murder.' He looked towards Gale. 'Do you plead guilty or not guilty as charged.'

'Not guilty,' aid Gale cheerfully. He winked at Mark.

And the case was on.

The prosecution was efficient but then, as Mark reminded himself, it would have been hard for them to be anything else.

They produced the gun, a small-calibre expanding bullet job, and gave evidence as to the cause of death. A doctor swore that he had removed the identified slug from the body. The police gave testimony as to the videophone call, the scene of the crime, the disposition of the body and the sets of fingerprints on the weapon. Finally, as if to make doubly certain, the prosecutor called Mark to the witness box.

'You are Mark Engles, Attorney-at-Law?'

'I am.'

'You were present in your office at the stated date and time of the crime?'

'Objection,' said Mark. 'I object to the use of the word 'crime'.'

'Objection overruled,' snapped the Judge. 'Continue.'

'Please answer my question,' said the prosecutor. Were you?'

'I was.'

'Did you see the accused shoot the alien known as Riphan?'

'I did.'

'Please describe to the Court exactly what took place.'

'I have said that my client shot the alien,' snapped Mark. 'Isn't that enough?'

'Please describe to the Court exactly what took place.' The prosecutor didn't smile but Mark could imagine what he felt like. As far as he was concerned the trial was a farce and should have been over long ago. Mark wondered if he really deserved the contempt in the other's eyes.

'The accused and myself were talking in my office, Mark said. 'Riphan came in and joined the conversation. We talked a while and then Riphan made as if to leave. Gale, my client, called to him. Riphan stopped and the accused took a gun from his pocket and shot him. He threw the weapon towards me, I caught it, and then called the police.'

Even as he spoke Mark knew what the prosecution were after. No possibility of self-defence. No possibility of accident. Nothing but a premeditated, cold-blooded killing.

'Thank you, Mr. Engles. Was Riphan carrying any sort of a weapon? A cane, for example? A heavy bottle? Anything like that?'

'No, the hands were empty.'

'Thank you. That will be all.' The prosecutor turned towards the Judge. 'That is the case for the prosecution, your Honour.'

'Defence?' The Judge looked as though he had a bad taste in his mouth.

'The defence is simple. your Honour,' said Mark and wished that he could get rid of the butterflies in his stomach. 'I move that the case be dismissed.'

'Dismissed?' The Judge glared at the young lawyer. 'On charge as one of murder. My client has not committed murder. Therefore there is no case for him to answer.'

'Ridiculous!' The Judge purpled beneath his wig. 'You yourself have admitted that you saw the accused kill a man in cold blood. Are you trying to be humorous at the expense of the court?'

'No, your Honour,' said Mark patiently. 'And I must correct your statement. I did not state that I had seen the accused shoot a man. I said that I had seen him shoot an alien.' Mark took a deep breath. 'According to statute 'murder' is defined as the unlawful killing of a human being with malice aforethought. Riphan was not a human being. Therefore my client cannot be charged with murder. On behalf of my client I wish to claim fifty thousand credits for wrongful arrest and imprisonment, and that he be allowed to leave this court without further hindrance.'

The following silence was merely the lull before the storm.

★ ★ ★

'Smart,' said Gale admiringly. 'That bit about the fifty thousand, I mean. Think you'll get away with it?'

'No, but it will give them something to worry about.' Mark sighed as he relaxed in his chair. The court had been adjourned following the bombshell and Mark guessed that the prosecution were busy trying to dig up some more evidence. He looked at Gale.

'You knew this all the time, didn't you?'

'Naturally.' Gale chuckled. 'You've got to be smart in this world, boy. I figured out that I could knock off one of the blue-skins and get away with it a long time ago. But I wanted to be paid for doing it and, more important, I wanted to make sure that I wouldn't be flung to the wolves. You filled the bill for the second part of the problem.'

'And Trans-Solar the first?' Mark narrowed his eyes at the fat man's expression. 'I had Vernon checked, it wasn't hard to find out who he worked for. What I want to know now is why he agreed to back you at all?'

'Maybe he liked the colour of my eyes,' said Gale blandly.

'Or maybe they want the aliens to get so disgusted with us that they'll go back where they came from and ignore us from now on? Is that it?'

'I wouldn't know,' said Gale easily. 'Anyway, what's it to you? You'll get paid.'

'Sure, I'll get paid and the whole planet will be flung back a thousand years,' said Mark bitterly. Looking at the fat man Mark realized just how he had been used as a catspaw. The entire set-up had been designed by the entrepreneur for his own ends. The partnership swindle to involve the lawyer, the witnessed shooting and veiled threats to make him act as the defence, Vernon to supply the money and to stand by to give hints as to what line the defence should take. That hadn't been necessary, Mark had thought it out for himself, but he didn't feel proud of it.

'That case,' said Gale suddenly. 'The one I asked you to take care of for me, have you got it?'

'I've got it.'

'Better get it handy. I'll want it as soon as I get out of here.'

'Is it that important?' Mark looked thoughtfully at the fat man. 'That partnership contract you signed with Riphan. Where is it?'

'Safe, Why?'

'I want it.'

'You'll get it,' promised Gale. 'After the trial.'

'I want it now,' snapped Mark. 'If I don't get it I don't go back into court. And don't try to threaten me. Your defence will work just as well for me as it will for you. Well?'

For a moment Gale hesitated, then he shrugged. 'All right, why not? You've played straight with me so far and I guess you can be trusted. I'll videophone one of my boys to pick it up. Take about an hour, that all right?'

'I want it before I go into Court.'

'You'll get it,' snapped Gale. For a moment he looked ugly.

'And don't forget that case.' He waddled towards a videophone booth as Mark left the room.

Outside Mark paused as John Morgan, thin nose held high, passed him as if he were dirt. Mark could sympathize with how the old man felt and, for a moment was tempted to follow him and explain. He fought down the impulse. Justice, to the President of the Bar Commission, was something too precious to be balanced on the meaning of a word. At least it was now, though in his younger days Mark suspected that he hadn't been above a little legal trickery himself. To hell with him.

A group of Lomians were talking to some reporters and Mark caught a snatch of what they were saying.

' . . . the Federation of course has laws designed to meet divergent life-forms. A defence such as we have seen here would not stand for one moment.'

'If the defendant is acquitted what will you do?'

'Naturally such an acquittal will make a great difference to our regard for your race. After all, how would you feel if one of your number was slain in cold blood by one of us?'

And that, thought Mark grimly, was the big money question.

10

The court convened and the procession of experts began. The prosecution had done a good job in the short time they had had at their disposal but, as one expert after the other rose to testify to the humanness of the Lomians, so one of Mark's shot him down.

Blood? It was blue, wasn't it? A lobster had blue blood, was a lobster human? Biped? An ape was biped, was an ape human? Talking? A parrot could talk, was a parrot human? Hands? A chimpanzee had hands, was a chimpanzee human? Ability to reason? A dog had that, was a dog human?

The prosecution didn't stand a chance.

Logic, thought Mark grimly. Cold, reasoned logic the only thing the evaluator accepted. Never mind the fact that the aliens belonged to a galactic wide Federation. Never mind that they had crossed light-years of emptiness to contact the human race and open vistas of trade and interchanged thought. They weren't human in the strict meaning of the word. They were easy game in a perpetual open season to any nut with a gun.

He stepped forward as the last of the witnesses left the stand.

'May it please the Court,' he said formally. 'Has the prosecution rested its case?'

'It has,' growled the prosecutor. He was sweating and had long lost his bland calmness.

'Does the defence wish to finalize?' The Judge glanced hopelessly at the evaluator. It was getting late but no one thought of adjourning until the next day. Everyone wanted this thing settled.

Mark smiled as he saw the direction of the Judge's glance.

'Yes, your Honour.' He paused for effect. 'It has been said that justice is not so much protecting the guilty as protecting the innocent. Conversely, should we protect the guilty and prosecute the innocent? Before the clerk closes the evaluator there is one point I would like to make clear. The defence, as you know, has rested on the fact that the slain creature was not a human being. It is a valid defence. It is valid, and will remain valid, unless it can be shown that the slayer of that creature both regarded and treated the creature as a man. I propose to prove that my client, Gale Hardin, did so consider his victim.'

'One moment.' The Judge leaned down from his bench. 'Am I to understand that you are now acting for the prosecution?'

'If it please the Court, that is my intention.'

'You can't do it,' shouted Gale. Guards grabbed him as he lunged forward. 'Mark, if you do it I'll take you with me. I swear it!'

'I realize,' said Mark evenly, 'that I am guilty of unethical behaviour. I also realize that I am in some personal danger. I ask the Court to remit my brief from the defendant.'

'Request granted,' said the Judge promptly. 'Clerk, order a lawyer to represent the interests of the defendant.' He smiled down at Mark. 'You may proceed.'

'I have in my hand a document inscribed and sworn by me in my capacity as an accredited witness for the administering of oaths.' Mark handed the partnership contract to the prosecutor.

'You will notice that the form is complete aside from the date. That is unimportant. Intent, in the eyes of the law, is as important as execution. I claim that the defendant freely, and without compulsion, entered into a partnership contract with the deceased.' He paused. 'I claim that he would not have done that unless he considered the deceased a man both as regards legal status and business standing.'

'Did you warn the defendant that the deceased had no legal status and so his contract would be invalid?' The Judge hadn't yet lost his smile.

'I did. His reply was that it didn't matter.' Mark glanced at the prosecutor. 'I need hardly emphasize the inference of this contract.'

He was right. Once again the experts paraded but this time the answers were all on the other side.

Would a man enter into a partnership with a dog? An ape? A lobster? A chimpanzee? A parrot? Partnership supposed equal rights and equal responsibility. You couldn't have one without the other and, if you admitted equal rights, then killing such a partner was murder no matter how the dictionary defined the exact meaning of the word.

The lie detector wrapped it up in a nice, neat bundle. Gale, swearing threats and screaming at his guards, was carried away to wait for immolation. Mark, his head still aching from the electrodes, waited for the Court to blast his career and send him to jail. The only bright spot he could see was that Gale had lied about his conditioning. He had told the truth, the whole truth, and nothing but the truth like it or not and, aside from the initial malpractice, Mark was in the clear.

He hoped that he could stay that way.

★   ★   ★

Morgan was very kind, he even smiled as Mark entered the room and the four

Lomians didn't seem to hate him at all. The other individual in the room was a member of the World Council, Mark recognized him from the gilt insignia he wore on his collar. He started the proceedings.

'Mr. Engles, the Lomian delegation wish to express their appreciation for what you have done. I need hardly say that it can only match our own. That was a great thing you did out there.'

'Great?' Mark shrugged. 'I merely sold my client down the river, that's all.'

'Justice triumphed,' said Morgan sonorously. 'My boy. I'm proud to call you a fellow member of a great profession.'

'Wait a minute,' said Mark. His head was aching so that he didn't seem to be able to think straight. 'First you hint that unless I played it your way I would be made to suffer for it. Well, I didn't play it your way. I went all out for an acquittal and would have got one as easy as falling off a log.'

'You would,' said Morgan. 'A very skilful defence indeed.'

'Right,' said Mark. 'So if that was good

then what do you call it when I turn round and send my client to immolation? Unethical, sure, but is that all you call it? What about integrity? What about my reputation? What about Gale? He's got a right to file a complaint against me and make it stick. If we're going to have justice let's have it all along the line. Fixing went out with the petrol engine.'

'I will admit that what you did was not in the best tradition of law,' said Morgan slowly. 'But circumstances alter cases. Hardin was not a nice man, he was a criminal who tried to use you and abuse the law for personal gain. He was also a thief.'

'A thief?'

'The Lomians inform me that certain papers were missing from Riphan's effects,' said the man from the World Council. Hardin took them, we discovered that through the lie-detector, but we don't know where they are.' He looked at Mark. 'You do.'

'No I don't.'

'You know how they can be obtained.'

'Yes.' Mark rubbed his aching head.

Lie-detectors blanked out the conscious and operated direct from the subconscious. The man being questioned had no memory of the incident but, because of that, could offer no information. All answers were on the yes-no basis. They knew he had access to the papers but, as he didn't know himself where they were, he couldn't have told them.

'The Lomians want those papers,' said the man from the World Council firmly. 'You must give them up.'

'Sure,' said Mark. 'I'll get them for you.' He stared at the tips of his fingers. 'No prosecution?'

'None.'

'No blame for unethical behaviour or malpractice?'

'Certainly not,' boomed Morgan. 'You leave here without a stain on your character.'

'Is that all?' Mark looked dubious. 'I was hoping for big things from this case.'

'All right, Engles,' said the man from the World Council. 'You know more than we thought. Those papers are dynamite. If you've examined them you know what

I'm talking about and if you haven't then I'm not going to explain. What do you want?'

'Are the Lomians going to stay with us?'

'Yes. We signed an agreement to join the Federation an hour after the verdict.' He looked grim. 'It was that close. Had the verdict gone the other way we would have lost our only chance at joining.'

'Good.' Mark paused. 'As we can expect quite a lot of aliens in the next few years, not to speak of our own people travelling to the stars, I guess that there would be room for a lawyer who knows all the ropes.' He smiled at the Lomians. 'I want a full education in Federation Law.'

'Is that all?' The World Councillor seemed relieved. 'Hell, that's no trouble. You've already been invited to help draft the new legislature to deal with extra-solar affairs. When can we have the papers?'

'Tomorrow morning.' Mark glanced at his wristwatch. 'I mean this morning. Say about ten at my office. That do you?'

'It will do.' The World Councillor seemed amused. 'Incidentally, don't try to have them photocopied. If you do you'll bleach them blank. The Lomians used a special ink which reverts when exposed to brilliant lighting.' He smiled at Mark's expression. 'If you should already have tried that, never mind, the blank paper will do. Until ten then, Mr. Engles.'

Mark nodded and walked out of the room. Vaguely he regretted a lost opportunity but, as he walked, the regret vanished.

Mark Engles, Attorney-at-Law sounded good. Mark Engles, Interstellar Counselor, sounded a lot better.

He could hardly wait to get into practice.

THE END

FIFTY DAYS TO DOOM
THE DEATH ZONE
THE STELLAR LEGION
STARDEATH
TOYMAN
STARSLAVE
S.T.A.R. FLIGHT
TO DREAM AGAIN

We do hope that you have enjoyed reading this large print book.

Did you know that all of our titles are available for purchase?

We publish a wide range of high quality large print books including:
Romances, Mysteries, Classics
General Fiction
Non Fiction and Westerns

Special interest titles available in large print are:
The Little Oxford Dictionary
Music Book, Song Book
Hymn Book, Service Book

Also available from us courtesy of Oxford University Press:
Young Readers' Dictionary
(large print edition)
Young Readers' Thesaurus
(large print edition)

For further information or a free brochure, please contact us at:
Ulverscroft Large Print Books Ltd.,
The Green, Bradgate Road, Anstey,
Leicester, LE7 7FU, England.
Tel: (00 44) **0116 236 4325**
Fax: (00 44) **0116 234 0205**

Other titles in the
Linford Mystery Library:

CAST A DEADLY SHADOW

Steve Hayes and David Whitehead

Four men went up into the mountains in search of a lost mine. Only one came back — insane with fear. Old Colonel Fogarty wanted to know what happened. No one seemed willing to find out, except his daughter, Rachel. She was joined by the colonel's mean-tempered surveyor, Harvey Wheeler, two locals with their own larcenous plans . . . and Jason Hart, a stranger whose job was 'chasing shadows'. But what were his intentions when the mountain's dark secrets were finally unlocked?